Breaking the Silence

Larry O'Loughlin is a storyteller and author of nine books for younger children; he is also co-author of *Our House*, a non-fiction book for adults. One of his titles for younger children, *The Gobán Saor*, illustrated by John Leonard, was shortlisted for the 1997 Bisto Book of the Year Award. His first book for teenagers, *Is Anybody Listening?* (published by Wolfhound Press in 1999), was short-listed for the 2000 Bisto Book Awards and was awarded a White Raven. Larry lives in Dublin with his wife and family. He is the father of award-winning teenage author Aislinn O'Loughlin, with whom he co-authored *Worms Can't Fly*, a book of poetry for younger children.

For victims and survivors everywhere

Breaking the Silence

Larry O'Loughlin

WOLFHOUND PRESS

First published in 2001 by
Wolfhound Press Ltd
68 Mountjoy Square
Dublin 1, Ireland
Tel: (353-1) 874 0354
Fax: (353-1) 872 0207

The Arts Council
An Chomhairle Ealaíon

Wolfhound Press receives financial assistance from The Arts Council/An Chomhairle Ealaíon, Dublin, Ireland.

British Library Cataloguing in Publication Data
A catalogue record for this book is available from the British Library.

ISBN 0-86327-836-1

10 9 8 7 6 5 4 3 2 1

Cover Illustration: Slide File
Cover Design: Slick Fish Design, Dublin
Typesetting: Wolfhound Press
Printed in the UK by Cox & Wyman Ltd, Reading, Berks.

'Feelings that are buried are buried alive.
They'll come back to haunt you.'

Don Baker, musician, actor and author

1

When they come, there are three of them.

The first grabs the boy's arms and pushes them high up his back, forcing him to bend so far forward that his face is just inches away from the floor of the shower.

The second pulls a rolled wet towel hard around his mouth, twisting it so tight he can hardly breathe.

For a moment the third does nothing. He's just there, silent, behind him. But the boy feels his presence, standing there, menacing.

Then he leans forward, places his mouth beside the boy's ear and chuckles.

'Welcome to the big boys, Declan.'

❑

Declan woke still dreaming, a strange half-strangled word-sound coming from deep in his throat, as he sat bolt upright and stared into the dark. His breath came in short, panic-filled gasps; he swung his arms, trying frantically to break their grip on him.

Somewhere, a dog barked.

The sound landed in his dream. It made tiny ripples that grew slowly bigger, drawing him into wakefulness.

The sense of relief moved through his whole body, relaxing it, bringing a feeling of calm. He stopped moving. Gradually he became aware of the warmth of the blankets against his skin, the softness of the bed beneath his body.

A dream — thank God!

But the relief didn't last. The calm was gone faster than a finger-click, transformed into disappointment. *That bloody dream, again!* He could have handled any other nightmare, but this one had been haunting him for three years.

He lifted his hand, reached up, and grabbed the corner of his bedroom curtain. The light from the street-lamp pierced into his room, and he fell back onto his pillow.

❏

The dream had started the night they first came for him. He'd woken, sitting up, screaming at the top of his voice, to find his parents looking down at him, their faces masks of concern.

'Are you OK, Dec?'

He couldn't tell them, not the truth. He couldn't tell anyone. That was the code: what happens in the locker room stays in the locker room. So he lied.

'Just a bad dream.' He forced an embarrassed smile. Even the smile was a lie, just there to convince them there was nothing to worry about.

They believed him. His father laughed with obvious relief. 'Thank God for that. The way you were screaming, I thought the banshee had come for me, and I'm not ready to meet my maker just yet.'

Declan laughed with him.

His mother hadn't laughed. She'd just lowered her head and kissed him on the forehead.

'You're all right now, love.' She'd ruffled his hair, as she had when he was a child. 'You're all right now.'

Declan had nodded and watched them go.

Somehow, after that first time, he'd managed to control the screaming, turn it into that muted word-sound. Unlike a scream, the strange sound didn't travel beyond his bedroom walls. So no one knew that for the next six months he'd woken every night, shaking in terror, his whole body covered in perspiration.

Then, gradually, it had come less often: every other night, then every week, every month, every few months, then not at all.

Declan had convinced himself it had gone forever, just disappeared to wherever bad dreams go when they don't come any more. But it hadn't. Six weeks earlier, it had come screaming back as he lay on his bedroll in the camp in Nepal. He'd woken to find Kumar and Mary standing over him.

'Bad dream?' Kumar had asked.

Declan had just nodded.

'They happen,' said Mary.

'Particularly if you're carrying a secret,' Kumar had whispered as Mary left.

Declan already knew that.

It had been coming every week since then — sometimes just once, sometimes twice.

And he hated it.

❑

He swung his legs over the side of the bed. For a second he just sat there, feeling hollow, staring at his feet. It was all he had the energy to do. Then he pushed himself up and walked out of his bedroom across the hall to the bathroom.

Getting his underwear off wasn't easy; he was covered in perspiration, and his T-shirt and briefs were clinging to him.

Eventually he won the battle; he let the underwear slip onto the floor, turned towards the shower and reached for the switch.

Then the anger hit him.

Declan spun around, kicking out angrily at the small pile of underwear at his feet. He sent it flying through the air. It slapped against the bathroom window and fell into the sink.

Bastards! he screamed silently. *Bastards! Even in my dreams they've got me!*

He turned and slammed his fist into the bathroom wall. It was an outside wall, solid concrete blocks covered in thin plasterboard. He pounded at it with his bare fists. His hands stung from the impact but he couldn't stop. He kept punching hard, over and over and over again, wishing that every punch were being delivered straight into the faces of Jason Meade and his friends.

Then he heard a soft tapping on the bathroom door.

'Declan? Declan, are you OK?'

His mother.

He couldn't believe he'd been that stupid. His parents' bedroom was right next to the bathroom: the noise was bound to wake one of them. *Thoughtless prat.*

'Sorry, Mam — I just slipped, but I'm OK now. Sorry to wake you.'

'That's OK, love. I was up anyway,' she fibbed back. 'Old habits die hard. I'll go down and put the kettle on.'

Declan listened to her walking slowly downstairs, and checked his watch. 6.50am.

Five years earlier, Rose Donnelly would have been out of the house and working at her job as an office cleaner by six-thirty. Sean, Declan's father, would have been out too, getting ready to drive a number 12 bus through Dublin's increasingly heavy traffic. But then Sean had had a triple heart bypass, and they'd both retired. Now they normally stayed in bed until after eight.

'Thoughtless prat,' Declan mumbled to himself. 'She doesn't need this.'

He took the small pouch from around his neck and placed it on the floor, then stepped into the shower. He held his face to the soft jet of water. He let it run over his chin and trickle down his body, let it wash away any last remnants of the dream.

Dream? He didn't know whether you could have flashbacks in your sleep; if you could, then that was what it was, a flashback, exact in every detail. The fear, the panic, the shame — it was all there. Only the pain was missing. That only came when he was awake, creeping up on him unexpectedly — sometimes out of nowhere, sometimes after seeing them, sometimes after he'd had the dream....

His stomach began to cramp. A dull, sickening pain started between his legs and spread all the way to his chest, making him gag. He bent double and leaned against the wall of the shower for support.

He was determined not to give in. He breathed in; bringing slow deep breaths right into the bottom of his stomach. He forced himself to visualise his breath moving gently around his body, softly calming each pain and ache. Slowly, the pain began to ease, just as he had known it would.

He straightened up. He poured shampoo onto his hands and rubbed it into his hair. His hands hurt, but it would have been worth the pain if it had actually been Meade, Cahill and O'Connor he'd been hammering. But what good would beating them do? It wouldn't take away what had happened. It wouldn't change the fact that they'd destroyed his life — not on that first night; later, on the second night, That Night. On the first night they'd just ruined everything.

He should have been able to look back on that night with joy and pride. He'd made school history — the first third-year ever chosen to play basketball on the senior team. It should have been one of the happiest memories of his life, but it wasn't. They'd made sure it wasn't.

For months after it happened, he'd tried not to think about it. Then he'd found a way to remember without the memories scaring him. He'd made that night unreal. He'd made it into a film he'd once seen, or an old video he'd taped off the television. Seeing it like that protected him.

❑

The boy is tall for his age. At six feet three inches he's tall for any age, but particularly tall for not-quite-fourteen. Sometimes, because he is head and shoulders taller than the other third-years, he walks with a slight stoop that makes him look awkward, even clumsy; but anyone watching him on the basketball court that night sees that he is far from awkward. He moves with the ease and grace of a natural athlete. And if he's over-awed to be playing with and against boys four and five years older than him, he doesn't show it. He plays with confidence and authority, helping his team to a comfortable win.

Later, in his post-match talk, Bob Fitzsimons, the coach, singles the boy out for praise.

'Welcome to the big boys, Declan. When Doc asked me to jump you up two teams, I had my doubts, but you've proved him right.'

Doc — Kieran Docherty — slaps the boy on the shoulder, and some of the others in the team shout 'Yeah!' and 'Well done.'

The coach turns and looks at three of the older players.

'Mr Meade, Mr O'Connor and Mr Cahill — you could all learn a lot from Declan's unselfish play. That's how I want to see you playing from now on. This is a team game. If you want to be solo stars, try boxing.'

The rest of the team smile and wink at the boy. Meade and O'Connor and Cahill just glare at him.

And later, they come at him.

❑

Declan heard the sound of cups being rattled downstairs, and then his mother singing to herself:
'Hush, little baby, don't say a word,
Momma's gonna buy you a mockingbird....'
He smiled. It was the song she'd sung him to sleep with when he was a baby. He guessed he always would be her baby, her little surprise; the baby who'd arrived long after she'd thought her child-rearing days were over.

'And there we were,' he remembered his father telling him, years and years before. 'Me and Mam, sitting there watching Christy and Marie and baby Darragh and all our other grandchildren playing a game, when I suddenly thinks to myself: "Wouldn't it be grand to have another little chiseler all of our own?" And do you know what happens then?'

'What?' Declan would ask, even though he'd heard the story a thousand times.

'There's this knock at the door, and when I open it, there stands the stork with this bundle in his beak! "Mr D," sez he to me, "we produced one too many babies at the baby factory. Would yous by any chance like a fresh one?" "I would," sez I. So I gave him fifty pence, and that's how we got ya. And do you know what day that was?'

'What day?'

'It was Christy's tenth birthday, and I had a hell of a job stopping him from taking you home as a present.'

The story always made Declan smile. His father had been fifty when Declan arrived, and his mother hadn't been far behind. All their other children were adults; three of them were already married, with children of their own. So when Declan had arrived, on his nephew Christy's tenth birthday, he was already an uncle six times over. He had never felt lonely as a child. There had always been some niece or

nephew — normally Darragh, who was nearest his age —
staying over with him. How he wished he could go back to
those times.

Declan shivered; he quickly turned off the water and
wrapped himself in a bath towel. Then he bent down, picked
the pouch up off the floor and hung it around his neck.

He'd never told anyone what they'd done to him that first
night. He'd almost told Christy, but he hadn't.

Christy and Darragh had been there the night it happened, watching the match, cheering every time Declan even
touched the ball. After the game Christy had driven them
home. Declan had hardly spoken a word in the entire journey; when they got home he'd gone straight to bed, pleading
tiredness.

They'd all seemed to believe him; but after a few minutes
the door to his bedroom had been pushed open and Christy
had walked in. He sat down on the edge of the bed.

'What'd they do tonight?' he asked sympathetically.
'Jump you in? Piss on you or shove soap up your arse when
you were in the shower?'

'That's a horrible word,' Declan replied, turning to face
the wall so Christy wouldn't notice he'd been crying.

'Arse? That's not rude,' laughed Christy. 'I'll have you
know, it's an old Anglo-Saxon word. God forbid that I
should use a rude word, and me almost a priest!'

'I don't care if it's rude or not,' said Declan, hoping his
voice wouldn't betray him. 'I just hate the sound of it.'

For a few seconds he didn't say anything else. Then,
without turning around, he answered Christy's original
question.

'Yeah, there was some jumping-in thing. It happens.'

He tried to sound casual about it but couldn't.

Christy didn't appear to notice. 'You're right. It does
happen, even to us wrestlers, even at college. It's meant to be
good-humoured, just a bit of fun, but sometimes it goes too

far. If anyone hurt you, you just tell me and I'll kill 'em. No one messes with my kid uncle.'

He ruffled Declan's hair. 'I mean it.'

Declan knew he did.

There'd been no humour in what Meade & Co. had done to him. It had been done out of spite. The coach had praised Declan and then immediately reprimanded them in front of everyone else. Their macho honour had been offended. They'd done what they had as their way of letting Declan know that, whatever happened out on the court, whatever anyone said, they were still top dogs and he was just some uppity kid.

The thought of seeing Meade and friends beaten to a pulp was so appealing that for a moment he'd been really tempted to tell, but he hadn't. That was the code....

Declan went into his bedroom, dropped the towel and began to dress, quickly. As he did he looked at himself in the full-length mirror: six foot five inches, lean frame with broad shoulders, solid arms and legs, slim waist — the body of an athlete, a swimmer or a film hero, and a scared little kid.

The dream always left him feeling scared; after a while the fear would pass and the hollowness would come.

He finished dressing and went down to the kitchen. His mother was sitting at the breakfast bar, drinking a cup of tea and doing the crossword in an old television guide.

'The tea's lovely and fresh, and the kettle's still warm, if you'd prefer coffee,' she said, looking up.

Declan poured a cup of tea and sat down at the table.

'Well, how are you this morning?' she asked. 'You look a bit pale. Are you all right?'

'I'm fine,' smiled Declan. 'Sorry I woke you. I didn't wake Dad, did I?'

'That fella? Since he retired, you could have the band of the US Marines parading through the bedroom and he wouldn't even budge.' Rose glanced down at the crossword again. 'Will you get yourself some cereal, love? I'm stuck on five down: six letters, "automobile dear", begins with a C.'

Declan shook his head. 'I'll leave you to it. I'm hopeless at crosswords.'

He poured himself a bowl of cereal, but he couldn't eat it. He looked at his mother. She didn't look sixty-four; but, then again, what did sixty-four look like? In the camp he'd met people the same age as his parents, or even younger, but they'd all looked old. He never thought of Rose and Sean as old; but then, they'd never been forced to flee their home-land, leaving everything they'd ever worked for behind them.

He missed the camp. He couldn't wait to get back. Instinctively, he touched his shirt, feeling the pouch that hung around his neck. Kumar had given it to him on his last day in Nepal. Then it had contained little pieces of earth from Bhutan and the camp in Nepal. Declan had added a little piece of earth from the Dublin Mountains and mixed them all together, so they'd never be separated.

He stared at his breakfast, stirring it absent-mindedly. He couldn't even really see the kitchen. All he could see was the dream, the same scenes over and over again, like a video loop. *Welcome to the big boys, Declan.... Welcome to the big boys....* He had to get away.

'I have to go. I have to do a few things before school,' he said standing up and quickly kissing his mother on the cheek.

'But you haven't touched your breakfast.'

'I have some money. I'll pick up a breakfast roll in a shop. Bye.'

2

'Two at once. Two at once.' Tommy Carolan repeated the words like a mantra as he ran down the stairs, taking them two at a time. He had to get to the kitchen first, before anyone could find what he'd hidden. No one else seemed to be awake yet, but he raced anyway.

He reached the refrigerator and opened the door. He hoped he wasn't already too late. Someone else could have got up in the night and taken it.... He knelt down and stretched his hand towards the back of the lower shelf.

'Oh, damn!'

It wasn't there!

For a few seconds he groped around the bottom shelf, his panic mounting. What if someone had taken it?

Then he sighed with relief as his hand touched the small Lucozade bottle. It was lying on its side. It must have been knocked over after he'd hidden it there the previous night.

'Yes!'

It felt nice and cool. He took the bottle out of the fridge, and smiled. The yellow liquid reached almost to the top. Tommy stood up, closed the door and looked at the clock on the kitchen wall.

7.45. He wasn't normally up this early. School was only a ten-minute walk away, and he didn't have to be in until nine, so he didn't usually surface until somewhere between eight-forty and eight-forty-five. But today was different. Today he had things to do. He needed to be up early.

The first thing he'd had to do was retrieve the bottle before anyone else found it. If Barbara had found it, she'd have guessed right away what he was planning to do; depending on her mood, she'd either have laughed or told their parents. If she had told, there would've been hell to pay. If either of his parents, or either of the twins, had found it and decided they needed a nice cool drink, there would have been a *lot* of hell to pay.

He found a packet of brown sugar and a teaspoon, and poured a neat teaspoonful of sugar into the bottle. He screwed the top back on and shook the bottle hard.

'Lovely,' he said, inspecting it proudly.

He put the bottle into the front pocket of his school-bag, and raced back upstairs to change from his pyjamas into his school uniform. It didn't take too long. His tie was still hanging around the neck of his shirt, and his shirt was still stuck inside his uniform pullover; so all he had to do was pick his pullover up off the floor and pull it over his head, and he was already half-dressed. Then he dragged off his pyjama bottoms and pulled his trousers on over his socks. He'd been wearing the same socks for four days and hadn't taken them off once. As he tightened his belt, he forced his feet into his still-laced shoes.

The whole process had taken less than fifteen seconds, but by the time Tommy emerged from his room the morning queue for the bathroom had already started. Nine-year-old Martin was banging on the door, telling his twin, Stacy, to get out before he went to the toilet on the floor. Barbara, who was seventeen, was relying on her big-sisterly charm: 'Get out before I kick the door down!'

Tommy didn't join them. He went back into the kitchen, turned on the tap, ran his hands under the water, and then rubbed them lightly around his face and over his hair. He dried them on his trousers.

He pulled a Vienna roll out of the bread-bin and broke a chunk off the end; then he opened the fridge, took the lid off the soft butter, and scooped up a huge blob of butter onto the bread. He closed the fridge door and sat on the edge of the kitchen table.

He looked at the clock. 8.00.

He was a boy with a mission. He'd been nominated by the rest of the second-year basketball team to try and talk Declan Donnelly into coaching them, and he was determined to succeed. Declan had coached them for their first term in secondary school, but he'd disappeared after the Christmas holidays and hadn't come back until a few weeks ago, after the first half-term of the new school year. That was ten months he'd been missing, and not one person Tommy knew had a clue where he'd been.

The school rumour mill, of course was full of stories: Declan was in jail, he'd joined a Buddhist monastery in Cavan, he was in a psychiatric hospital, he was in rehab for a secret drug problem. One rumour even had him on the run from drug dealers. A variation on that one had him receiving plastic surgery and being relocated somewhere abroad as he waited to give evidence against some drug baron.

Tommy didn't believe any of them. His guess was that Declan had just taken off somewhere, to try and get over what had happened to his pal Doc.

When Declan disappeared, the team had been coached by a variety of seniors for the rest of their first year, and for the new school year they'd been assigned a coach from the fifth-year team, Michael Crean. He was a nice guy and not a bad player. If Declan hadn't come back, nobody would have been too unhappy with him; but Declan *was* back. At first the second-years had automatically assumed that he'd take up where he'd left off, both as a player and as their coach; but he hadn't. He hadn't shown any interest in basketball since he'd come back.

A couple of times, when Tommy and his pals had been practising in the yard after school, they'd seen signs of the old Declan. He'd run into the game and played along with them, laughing, encouraging them, really enjoying himself. Then, every time, he'd just stopped without warning and walked off. It was if he'd suddenly remembered he wasn't allowed to play with them, or something. Tommy had no idea what that was all about, and he didn't really care. He was determined to get Declan to coach them again. He'd been asking him nearly every day for three weeks. So far the answer had always been 'no', but Tommy reckoned Declan wouldn't keep that up forever. As he'd told the other second-years, 'You never see Declan hanging around with any of his old mates any more, or even talking to anyone, really. He's got to get bored of being a loner sometime. When he does, I'll be there.'

Tommy was going to ask him this morning and at break and at lunch and at home-time, and he might even get the Donnellys' number and call him at home.

'They've got a name for kids like you,' one of his mates had told him.

'What?' Tommy had asked. 'Enthusiasts?'

'No, stalkers.'

He finished the bread and was busy wiping his fingers on his jumper when the back door opened. His parents came in. They were both wearing running-shorts and vests and pro-fessional running-shoes. *Don't they know it's winter?* thought Tommy. He didn't usually see them dressed like this in the morning. He'd normally be still in bed.

'Well, good morning, starshine,' said his father, pretend-ing to aim a blow at Tommy's stomach. Tommy parried it.

'To what do we owe this honour?' asked his mother, closing the door behind her. She looked just like an older version of Tommy and his brother and sisters — red hair and freckles.

'I've got things to do before school,' he answered.

He opened his school-bag, reached into the back section and grabbed out a crumpled ball of black material, which he unfolded into his blazer. His father shook his head.

'What? What?' asked Tommy.

'I was just wondering how much money we'd save if we could buy them ready-crumpled.'

Tommy shot him a sarcastic smile, and pulled the blazer over his jumper.

'I hope you had breakfast,' said his mother.

'I certainly did,' lied Tommy. 'Muesli with extra wheat germ, toasted sesame seeds and pumpkin seed, all swimming in soya milk.'

'Good lad.'

He was never certain if she believed him, or if she knew that he was lying and just decided to play along anyway. She leaned over and ruffled his unbrushed red hair.

'Ah, Mam,' he said, pulling away. 'I've just spent ages getting that style, and now you've gone and ruined it.'

He grabbed his school-bag and looked in, double-checking that everything was there.

Two cans of Coke — check. Two cheese sandwiches — check. Two packets of crisps — check. Two Mars bars — check. (He didn't want to go hungry.) And an apple.

Sitting on top of all that was the Lucozade bottle.

'Right. See ya.'

He opened the back door and stepped out onto the path.

3

Declan stopped. A few yards away, a fox was moving cautiously among the stones. He didn't want to frighten it. So he waited, scuffing the toe of his shoe along the ground absent-mindedly, listening to the sound of the pebbles scrunching beneath his foot.

He had heard a story once. It was a story about a kid — an ordinary city kid, just like him, only younger. A plane had crashed in Northern Canada and the kid been the only survivor. For two months he'd wandered around in the wilderness, all alone: just him, the mountains, the rivers, and his thoughts of home.

And then he'd made it.

He'd stumbled into some village, and the people there had taken him in and flown him home — back to the city, back to his family, back to pick up the threads of his real life just where he'd left off.

The thing was, he couldn't do it.

Something had changed. He'd changed.

He couldn't take it any more, any of it: the buildings, the traffic, the people, the noise, the shops, the hanging around at the mall or playing games at the arcade. It made him feel claustrophobic and ill at ease. And it didn't matter how hard he tried; he couldn't fit in. All he wanted was to get back, back to the wilderness, back to the wild.

When Declan had left the camp, he thought he'd be able to handle Dublin. It had seemed so easy. It was only for eight months. All he had to do was keep his head down, keep away from Meade, shut everyone else out until June, and then he'd be back in the camp. It would only be for the summer; after that he'd have to come back for one more year at school, and then there'd be university. But all that was far away. All he had to do was make it till June. Surely he could do that?

He wasn't so sure now.

He bent down, picked up one of the pebbles and turned it over in his hand, feeling its cool, smooth roundness. For a second he thought about throwing it, but it would have been irreverent to disturb the peace. So he just held it in his hand, rubbing it between the inside of his thumb and the side of his finger. It made him feel calm, relaxed and at ease. This place always did.

It was his wilderness. No mountains, no rivers, no wild animals — apart from the odd city fox — but it was a wilderness, and he'd been coming to it three, sometimes four times a week since he'd got home. At that time of the morning, he was usually the only one there. He liked that.

This morning, he needed his wilderness. School could wait.

The fox had gone. Declan passed along the straight, perfectly manicured path, listening to the pebbles scrunching under his feet. At the bottom of the path he turned right, then left onto a smaller path. After a few feet he stopped. He took a can of Lucozade from the pocket of his leather jacket and pulled back the tab.

'Hi, Doc. How's it going? Sorry I haven't been around for a couple of days, but you know what it's like.'

He lowered himself onto the granite surround and leaned

back against the upright stone, raising the can in a salute. 'Cheers.'

He closed his eyes, holding the can out in front of him. He could see the tall dark-haired boy leaning forward, taking the can, having a quick drink and smiling across at him: 'Right, post-match analysis.'

That was their ritual; it always had been, ever since Declan's second game for the seniors. Every night, after a game or practice, they'd sit on the benches in the changing-room, sharing a Lucozade, replaying and analysing every move and score. The only night it hadn't happened was That Night.

'No post-match analysis today, Doc,' he said softly. 'I need to talk.'

He stopped and took a deep breath. 'I don't know if I can make it, Doc. I honestly don't. I just can't take all that crap they put us through. I could block it out in the camp, some-how — maybe because what they'd gone through was even worse, maybe because I was focused on the kids. I dunno. But I was OK there. But the moment I got off that plane in Dublin airport....'

He stopped and took another long swig from the can. He wanted to curl up, just go to sleep and forget about it all.

'God. They really did a number on us, didn't they, Doc?'

As soon as he'd said it, he wished he hadn't. Doc wasn't smiling any more. His head had dropped to his chest and he was staring at the floor, just as he had on That Night. The night they'd come for the second time.

❑

Doc is sitting just a few feet away. He is almost near enough to touch, but they might just as well be in different countries. Doc doesn't even acknowledge him. He just sits there, staring at the tiled floor of the changing-room. Declan sits next to the lockers, trying to think of some way to break that thick, poisonous silence.

'Doc. Doc, you OK?'

Doc doesn't reply.

'Doc, I'm really sorry.'

Declan moves along the bench. He places his hand on Doc's bare shoulder. Doc pushes his arm away and moves further along the bench. He continues to stare at the floor. Declan sits there, hoping he will look up and say something. He doesn't. Declan goes back to his spot, pulls his bare feet up onto the bench, tucks his knees under his chin and pushes his back against the side of the locker.

'Doc, I'm —'

'Just forget about it,' Doc snaps angrily. 'Just finish getting dressed and get out, go home.'

Declan feels the words like another punch. Doc has never spoken to him like that before. In the three years they have been team-mates and friends, the only times Doc has ever raised his voice to him have been to shout encouragement or cheer him on when he's scored a basket....

Declan picks up his polo-neck and pulls it over his head. He tugs his socks on and slips his feet into a pair of black cowboy boots that his brother Tony brought him back from San Antonio, Texas. All the time he is dressing he keeps his eyes firmly fixed on Doc. Doc doesn't move. He just sits, half-wrapped in a towel, staring at the floor.

If he ranted and raved, ran around kicking the lockers over, smashed the showers with one of the hurling sticks that are lying in the corner, Declan would understand. If he grabbed Declan by the hair and rammed him face-first into the wall, then Declan would know what to do, how to react. But the silence, this awful bloody silence — he has no idea what to do about that.

He wants to make the silence go away, to let things get back to the way they were before, but he can't. And that hurts. It hurts even more than his swollen, bloodied lip, the cut over his eye, the dull, sickening pain that starts between his legs and ends somewhere in his stomach.

He grabs the towel and rubs it quickly across his hair. He takes out his comb and walks slowly to the mirror at the end of the changing-room. And all the time he is watching Doc, urging him silently, Say something. Do something. Trip me, spit at me, curse out loud, but for God's sake do something.

Doc doesn't react.

Declan combs his hair, keeps careful watch on Doc's reflection in the mirror, waiting. Suddenly, Doc lifts his head. His eyes are closed. Without warning he slams his head hard against the backboard of the bench, with a crash. He raises his hands, clenches them together, and slams them hard against the clothes-hooks just above his head — once, twice, three, four times.

'Doc, don't.' Declan spins around to face him. 'Don't!'

Doc opens his eyes and stares at him. His eyes are dark, heavy, accusing.

'Don't talk to me,' he snaps.

Declan moves towards him. He reaches out his hand to touch him, but Doc angrily hits it away.

'Don't — don't touch me!' Doc is waving his arms in front of his face as he shouts. 'Don't touch me. Don't talk to me. Don't even look at me. Just go home. Leave me alone. Go on! Get out!'

'Doc, I —'

'Which part of "Get lost" don't you understand, Donnelly?' Doc screams. 'Just leave me alone!'

'But I can't go and leave you like this.'

'Oh, please! Take your guilt trip somewhere else.'

Declan stands there looking at him, staring into his deep, hurt eyes.

Then he scoops up his things, slings them into his bag, pulls on his coat and pulls the bag up onto his shoulder.

'Doc — let me give you a lift home. I've got my dad's car outside.'

'I don't want anything off you.'

'But you look like death, and —'

Doc looks at him. His eyes are cold and emotionless. Declan has to turn away.

'You weren't there when I needed you. Now I don't need anyone. So just get lost.'

Doc turns back to the floor. Declan walks slowly across the changing-room. At the door, he stops and turns around. Doc is leaning forward. His head rests in his hands and his whole body is shaking with silent sobs.

I did this to him!

Declan races out of the changing-room and down the corridor. He bursts through the door to the playground, yanks the car door open and throws himself onto the driver's seat. His whole body is shaking.

Declan puts his head against his arm and leans on the steering-wheel.

❑

Declan turned to look at the writing on the stone. *Kieran Docherty ... died 19 December, aged 20 ... beautiful spirit taken from us all too soon ... greatly missed by his parents, brother, sisters and friends....*

Almost a year.

Declan looked back across the field. There was no sign of the fox. He guessed it had reached safety. Maybe it was even telling the other foxes about their encounter. 'Hey, guys, guess what I just saw?'

He smiled briefly. Then he turned back to the grave.

'Why did you have to go and die?' he asked softly, the words almost catching in his throat. 'We could have worked

it out. We'd have got even with them somehow. But now ...
Meade and the others just keep winning.'

He stopped and shook his head slowly.

'Sorry for moaning. It's just — I really miss you, pal.'

He lay back against the headstone and closed his eyes,
breathing in the peace and quiet.

4

Tommy stopped beside the building site. He looked around, checking that there wasn't anyone coming. When he was sure he wouldn't be seen, he slipped behind a wild hedge. The hedge covered a small hole in the fence. He squeezed himself through the hole and came out into the site.

When he was younger, there'd been a small country pub on the spot. Behind the pub there had been a small orchard where the older kids had gone scrumping, stealing apples and pears from the trees. Then the people who owned the pub had decided to go modern. They'd extended the premises, building up and out. They'd added another bar upstairs and replaced the orchard with a car park. They'd made the whole thing bigger and posher. Now they were at it again.

Tommy looked at the mess of girders and concrete blocks in the side car park. In a few months they would be transformed into a cinema and hotel complex, just like the one on the notice-board inside the fence. Personally, he'd have preferred them to put the orchard back so he could go scrumping, but no one had asked him what he wanted.

He checked his watch. It was 8.15. The site was still quiet; work wouldn't begin for another fifteen minutes.

Tommy headed for a small fenced compound which the builders used for storing empty containers, used pallets and some small machinery. He squeezed through a small gap in the chained gates.

'Billy,' he called quietly. 'Bill.'

A group of pallets moved, and a small, bony hand emerged in from the gap. It was clutching a filthy tin mug.

'Hi, Tommy, want a cuppa?' said a voice. A cup of something brown and cold was pushed towards him.

'No, thanks, Bill. I've got to be there early today.'

'That'll be a bloody first.'

Another group of pallets were moved aside, and a figure emerged through the gap.

'I'm bloody freezing,' moaned Billy, and as if to prove a point he started coughing.

He was about the same height as Tommy, but thinner. He was wearing an ex-army parka with the insignia of the German army on the left sleeve. The parka swamped him, making him look even thinner. He kept the hood pulled up so that his face was barely visible.

'And how are you today, Kenny?' said Tommy, laughing. Billy didn't watch *South Park* any more — he didn't exactly have the choice — but Tommy knew he used to.

'Piss off!' replied Billy. He pushed the hood down, revealing tightly cropped blond hair. His face had a sickly grey pallor. He had a small scar on his cheek, another on his forehead and a longer one that ran from his ear to his jaw.

'I'll try to nick a few more things to keep you warm,' Tommy promised. He opened his bag. 'Here, I brought you a cheese sambo and a packet of crisps.'

He pushed them towards Billy. Billy took them eagerly.

He'd been living rough on the building site since shortly after work on the hotel had begun, three months earlier. Tommy had discovered him one night when he'd climbed into the site to go exploring. He'd nearly died. The cropped hair, the scars, and the fact that he was filthy gave Billy a fairly vicious look. But he'd been as scared as Tommy. They'd both shouted out in surprise, but Tommy had got over the shock faster. It had taken Billy days to trust him, but once he had, they became close. Tommy had never told anyone else about Billy. He'd promised he wouldn't. The less people who knew about him, the less chance there was that the wrong person would find him.

Tommy was his regular food-pusher. He'd never fished for any information, and Billy had never volunteered much. He was fifteen and he came from near the shopping centre. He'd left home to get away from his father's fists. At first he'd tried dossing down on friends' floors, but his dad had always managed to find him; he'd turn up drunk, swearing and threatening to wreck the gaff unless Billy was sent out. So Billy would leave with him, and when he got home the beatings would be worse than ever. He'd tried living on the streets around town for a while, but he wasn't tough enough to look after himself. He'd been beaten up a couple of times by some of the other kids on the street. He liked the site, though. It was safer than the streets, and Tommy was around.

Once, over a cuppa, Tommy had asked him what he'd do when the work on the site was finished or he was found out.

'Dunno. I'll cross that bridge when I come to it.'

Tommy couldn't even imagine what it was like.

Billy opened the cheese sandwich and started eating it hungrily. Then he sneezed. 'I've been at that all bloody night,' he said.

'I'll try and get you something for it later,' Tommy promised. 'But I have to head now. I'll see you later.'

'Yeah, bye. Bye.'

As he crossed the site, Tommy looked up at the roofless shell of the building. It was six stories high — a concrete base with huge, thick girders, vertical and horizontal, rising above it, criss-crossing to form the skeleton of the hotel. It looked like an X-ray. Once, he'd seen builders running along the girders, as if they were tightrope-walkers in a circus. They'd been carrying boxes of big bolts and nuts. Tommy had felt dizzy just watching them. How could anyone go up there? He wouldn't do it for a million pounds. He was scared stiff of heights.

He crossed the road and headed for school. The gates were already open. So he walked into the playground, positioned himself just beside the gates and sat down to wait for Declan.

He checked his watch. 8.55. The playground was filling up, and the street was full of kids heading towards the school. Tommy glanced up and down the road. No sign of Declan yet.

Then he spotted Jason Meade.

He was sauntering up the road towards the Senior Community College attached to the school, where he was repeating his Leaving Cert. exams for the second time. Students at the Community College weren't supposed to use the school entrance or enter the school buildings unless they were on some supervised activity — a lot of them, including Meade, were in the school basketball club — but that never stopped Meade.

Tommy took the Lucozade bottle out of his bag. Keeping one eye on Meade, he opened it and held it in his hand as if he was ready to drink it.

He was scared of Meade. Most of the younger basketball players were. A lot of the older guys teased the younger kids, hiding their clothes or putting liquid soap in their shoes, but Tommy reckoned that was just part of being in a club. It was just messing, nothing nasty. Meade was different. He enjoyed pushing kids' heads down toilets, or lashing them around with wet knotted towels, or grabbing them by the hair on the backs of their necks. The older guys tried to protect them, as much as they could, but everyone in the club was scared of Meade to some extent.

'So. What you doing, wimp?' laughed Meade as he came closer. 'Waiting for Godot?'

Tommy had no idea what he meant, but he laughed anyway. 'No, I'm just —'

'And you brought me a drink, too. How nice.'

Meade made a snatch at the drink. Tommy jerked it away, protecting it, but Meade just pushed him up against the fence and took it anyway.

'Thanks a lot, wimp!'

Tommy stood at the fence, watching Meade walk across the playground taking big swigs from the bottle. There were tears in his eyes, and he put his hand in his mouth and bit hard to stop the sounds building up in his throat. His shoulders shook.

'Creep's made Tommy cry,' said a group of the other second-years as they passed by. Tommy didn't say anything. He just waved them away and slunk to the ground, head down, his whole body shaking.

He watched Meade disappear around the corner towards the field that separated the school from the college. Then he couldn't control it any longer. He burst out laughing.

'Gotcha, you big *sap*!' he howled. 'Gotcha!'

As the bell for the start of classes sounded, he looked up and down the road. Still no sign of Declan. So he headed off across the playground, tears running down his cheeks as he laughed.

'Hey, wait up,' he called to a group of second-years walking ahead of him. They slowed down to let him catch up.

'Guess what I just did,' Tommy said when he joined them. They stopped to listen. 'See, Jason Meade was ...' He dropped his voice to a conspiratorial whisper.

A few seconds later, the whole group burst out laughing.

'*Sap*!' they chorused.

5

The sound of an engine startled Declan. He opened his eyes. On the far side of the cemetery, a mechanical digger was digging a new grave. He watched for a few seconds. The digger seemed out of place — some tired old animal clawing at the still earth of his wilderness.

He felt empty, almost hollow. He stretched and looked at his watch. 9.45.

He pushed himself up. 'I've got to go. I can't be late too often. The sooner I get all this over, the sooner it's summer and I can get back to the camp.'

He gave a short, ironic laugh. 'Great, huh? A hundred thousand people praying to get out of the camps and go back home to Bhutan, and here I am praying to get back in.'

He leaned forward and placed the half-full can of Lucozade on the grave.

'See you soon.'

As he reached the car park he turned around and looked at the cemetery. It was so peaceful, so restful, like a garden: a garden of stones.

❑

Fifteen minutes later, he was guiding his father's old Volkswagen through the main gates of the school.

Declan still found it strange to be back in school. For ten months he'd been a teaching assistant in the camp, working with the children, teaching them art and basketball. He smiled at that thought.

The basketball hadn't been part of any plan. It had just happened. On his third night there, Declan had found an old, spokeless bicycle-wheel. He nailed it to a tree and borrowed a ball to shoot some hoops. A small group of children gathered around to watch, so he invited them to join in. By the end of the night, nearly every kid in the camp was there. Declan divided them into teams and an *ad hoc* tournament developed. The following day, he'd cleared some scrub and marked out a rough court. Mary O'Dwyer, a teacher from Dublin who was working in the camp as a teacher-trainer, had found some old uprights and nets somewhere, and the games became organised — almost.

The kids weren't interested in the finer points of the game. They just charged around, bouncing into each other and throwing the ball in the general direction of the nets. Over the months, Declan managed to get some semblance of order into the game, but Mary still referred to it as 'Declan's basket-rugby-chaos'. Some of the other teachers called it 'mini-warfare'.

But no one had ever told him to stop. In all his time there, they'd never treated him as a kid. Mary might joke about 'having to wipe your nose for you', but she'd never once treated Declan as anything but a colleague, a work-mate. Kumar was the same: he was one of the camp leaders, and twenty years older than Declan, but he'd treated him as an equal, and Declan had viewed him as a combination of friend and honorary big brother. Now he was back in school. He was a schoolkid again. He was finding it hard to get used to the change.

He drove slowly past a row of cars parked in the main car park, keeping a careful lookout for the unexpected. Five weeks earlier he'd nearly run someone down there, a girl called Laura Byrne who was in his class. He'd been coming in late and hadn't been expecting to see anyone around. She'd just stepped out from between the parked cars and walked straight in front of him without looking. She hadn't even seen him. Fortunately he hadn't been going fast, but he'd still practically had to stand up on the brake to stop. He'd missed Laura by inches, but she hadn't even noticed. She'd just carried on walking across the yard, talking to herself. Then she'd stopped, stared upwards and started waving her hands around, shouting, as if she was arguing with something in the sky. Declan had looked up. There was nothing there. He hadn't really thought there would be.

She was really giving out hell to something.

Suddenly she'd glanced towards the school, smiled and run off. He looked to see what had attracted her attention. Three girls he'd seen her with — Sarah, Cass and Tina — were standing at the window. They were laughing and waving their arms around, making fun of Laura.

Declan's rush of anger — *Bitches!* — had taken him by surprise.

He'd warned himself, *It's got nothing to do with you, man. You just smile and nod at people, but you don't get too close, remember? That's your number one rule to help you get through to June.*

But he couldn't help it. Maybe there was a tiny crack appearing in his protective wall, because rule or no rule, he suddenly felt himself drawn towards Laura Byrne. One weirdo attracted to another?

A couple of days later she'd been rushed to hospital after a near-fatal asthma attack. She'd been absent for almost a month now. He missed seeing her around.

He turned left into the small car park at the rear entrance

and slipped the old Volkswagen between two parked cars. He pulled off his leather jacket, replaced it with his blazer, grabbed his school-bag, and headed across the playground in the direction of the students' entrance.

It was 10.15. The corridor was empty. Everyone was in class, or almost everyone.

❑

Tommy was sitting in his hiding-place under the stairs. He'd been there about fifteen minutes, long enough to finish one of his Mars bars and half a can of Coke. He was prepared to stay there all day if necessary. He lifted the can to his lips, but before he could take another sip the door opened. He peeped out from his hiding-place. Declan was walking down the corridor.

Tommy jumped to his feet. 'Declan, Declan,' he called, trotting down the corridor, breaking at least two school rules. 'Declan!'

Declan stopped. He looked up at the ceiling and smiled.

'Yes, Tommy.'

He didn't turn around right away. He didn't have to. He knew exactly what he'd see behind him: a red-haired kid with freckles, hair tossed as if it had never seen a brush, shirt hanging out front and back, more then likely pulling his school-bag along the ground with one hand and holding a sandwich in the other.

During Declan's first few days back, a lot of kids had tried to talk to him and include him in their groups of friends. He'd been polite and friendly but distant, and after a while they'd stopped trying. Now when they saw him they'd just nod and say 'Hi,' or maybe exchange a few polite words about nothing of any real importance. Other than that, they kept their distance and gave him his space. He liked that.

Tommy was the exception. Tommy never gave up. It

didn't matter how hard Declan tried to ignore him; he didn't seemed to notice. Declan wondered if he was practising to be a stalker when he got older. Every time he turned around, Tommy was there. It reminded him of the way he'd trailed after Doc after the first night.

'Declan, I've been waiting for you.'

Declan turned around. He smiled to himself. He'd been wrong about the sandwich. It was a can of Coke.

'Don't you ever go to classes?' he asked. 'Every time I look around, you're on the steps, eating or drinking. Did I miss something? Have second-years got a dispensation these days?'

Tommy didn't say anything. He wasn't even sure he knew what a dispensation was. He just smiled, and lifted his eyebrows.

Declan thought, *If the school ever decides to stage* Oliver, *this guy would make a perfect Artful Dodger.*

'You said I could ask you some other time about giving us some extra basketball coaching, and I thought if I asked you this morning we could start this afternoon,' Tommy garbled in one long excited breath.

'And when exactly did I say that?' asked Declan.

'When I asked you yesterday afternoon.'

'I'll tell you what, then. Ask me again in about a week. Maybe I'll be ready to start by then, and if I am, I promise you can be my first pupil.'

'Great, that's great,' said Tommy enthusiastically. 'I'll keep you to that.'

He pulled his bag up and clutched it under his arm. 'I'd better get back to the library. We're on a study morning. You never know, I might even learn something. See you.'

He turned around and headed off.

'He's definitely weakening,' Tommy said to himself. 'Definitely.'

Declan watched him walk towards the library, still

drinking his Coke. He was fairly certain of two things: Tommy wouldn't wait a week before he asked again; and he'd never play or coach again, not in Dublin.

Part of him wished he could. He liked Tommy, but he couldn't do it. He had to stay behind his wall, keep his head down until June, but it wasn't easy.

'Still got an eye for little boys, I see,' sneered a voice behind him.

Declan froze.

Meade.

He wasn't supposed to be in this part of the school, but that never seemed to bother him.

Declan felt a small knot of fear in the pit of his stomach. He tried to ignore it, just as he had whenever he'd seen Meade since he came back.

'Go and play with yourself some more, Meade,' he said, hurling the words over his shoulder. He didn't turn around. He didn't want to make eye contact. He just wanted to get away.

He started to walk off, hoping Meade wouldn't notice his hands shaking. Suddenly he felt a sharp slap on the buttocks and heard Meade laugh. He spun around. Meade was already making his way to the door to the playground.

'See you around, Deckie,' he smiled. Then he blew Declan a kiss.

Declan felt himself flush with anger, but before he could react Meade had slammed the door and was gone.

He screamed silently. He kicked the door to the changing-room, hard. It swung back and then sprang forward again. He kicked it a second time and heard it clatter back against the wall. He stormed into the changing-room. There was a medicine ball by the door; he picked it up and hurled it at one of the benches in pure rage. The ball landed with a dull thud. He leaned over, picked it up again and hurled it at the lockers. They shuddered.

The pain started in between his legs and spread to his stomach. It was a dull, sickening ache. He bent double, gagging, trying to breathe.

He pushed himself up and staggered across to the hand-basins. He filled one of the basins and plunged his head in the water. He kept it there for a few seconds. Then he lifted his head and sat down on a bench. The pain was easing. He put his head in his hands.

❑

The sound of the bell for the end of the period startled him. He forced himself up and washed his face in the hand-basin, drying it with paper towels. As he turned to throw the towels in the bin, the doors burst open in a clatter of noisy fourth-years. A couple of them greeted him with 'Hi, Dec, how's it going?' or just 'Declan,' others nodded, but most just ignored him.

As he moved towards the doors, they were suddenly pushed open.

'OK, you lot, quiet down. You've got two minutes to get changed and out into the gym, and no messing around.' The teacher's message was automatic. He didn't even look at the kids.

Declan pushed the door and stepped past.

'Declan.'

He turned. Bob Fitzsimons was standing at the door, dressed, as usual, in a tracksuit. A whistle hung from a ribbon around his neck and he held a clipboard.

'The very man. I was just coming to find you,' the teacher smiled.

'Hi, sir, how's it going?' Declan replied without smiling.

'Fine. Fine,' Bob Fitzsimons replied, tapping his pen against the clipboard. Then he stopped tapping and stared at Declan.

'How about you, Declan? How's it going for you since you came back?'

'Fine,' lied Declan, forcing a smile.

'How long have you been back now?'

'Six weeks. I came back late because ...' Declan let it trail off. He knew Bob wasn't actually looking for an answer. It was a rhetorical question.

Bob stared at Declan for a few seconds without saying anything. Declan looked away.

'Well, I reckon you can guess what the next part of my question is.'

'Why haven't I been to basketball training?' offered Declan.

'Precisely. I know it's voluntary and you have every right not to come, but I would still have expected to see you there.'

'I'd just be wasting your time, sir. Yours and everyone else's. I can't play any more.'

'You mean you've got something else to do?'

'No, sir, it's not that. It's just — well, the way I've been when I've tried it at home or with my friends ...' He didn't have any friends any more. 'I reckon you've got first-years who are better than me.'

'I doubt that,' laughed Bob. 'You're an inter-county player.'

'*Was*,' corrected Declan. 'Honest, sir, I'm not having you on. Whatever ability I used to have at basketball seems to have just gone with the wind.'

'Why not let me be the judge of that?' suggested Bob. 'Maybe you're just a bit rusty. After all, it's been nearly a year since you last played competitively. Why not come along tonight, even if it's only for fifteen minutes or so?'

'I'll just be wasting your time, sir.'

'Hey, I'm a teacher,' replied Bob, shrugging his shoulders. 'I get paid to have my time wasted. You can't waste it any more than this lot.'

He nodded to the boys getting changed noisily in the locker-room.

'Practice is at the same time as it always was. Half-eight, straight after badminton practice.'

'I can't tonight. Maybe next session or next week,' said Declan. 'I promise.'

'I'll see you then. Now you'd better get back to class.'

Declan turned to go.

'And, Declan —'

Declan turned around.

'I miss him too, you know, but I don't think Doc would want you to drop everything because of him.'

❑

It is a Monday, 19 December. Two days after That Night. It's just coming up to lunch hour. Declan is sitting in economics class, completing a multiple-choice test — 'Which letters are used to explain the Fisher Equation in its abbreviated form?' — when Bob Fitzsimons's voice comes over the school intercom.

'Will all members of the senior and junior basketball teams go immediately to the gym. That's all senior and junior basketball teams to the gym.'

Declan is the only basketball player in sixth-year economics. He looks at the teacher.

'Is it OK if I go, Miss?'

'You heard His Master's Voice,' she smiles. 'Off you go. You can hand in your paper; I doubt if you'll be back before lunch. He's never been known to make short announcements, has he?'

'Not that I remember,' Declan laughs as he puts the paper on her desk.

The other basketball players are piling out of their classes and heading down the corridor like a bunch of excited kids, glad of any excuse to get a few minutes out of class. No one has any idea why they've been called. Declan hears one of the fifth-years teasing Tommy and some of the other first-years: 'Maybe they're taking us on a secret trip to celebrate the fact you lot finally won a game last week.'

'Blame our coach,' grins Tommy, looking at Declan.

'Watch it, you,' Declan replies, ruffling Tommy's hair.

They open the doors to the gym and walk in, and almost immediately the chatter and laughter stop.

Bob Fitzsimons is standing at the far end of the hall. One look at his face tells them that whatever he has to say is no laughing matter. He looks grey-faced and sick.

'I've just received a phone call from Mrs Docherty, the mother of Kieran Docherty....' Then he has to fight back the tears.

There is a sudden sharp intake of breath from everyone in the room. They seem to know what is coming next. Declan feels himself turn cold. Everything seems to be happening in slow motion, and every word seems to bounce around the walls, echoing louder and louder.

'Doc was killed in a car crash on his way to college this morning.'

The silence becomes even more intense. Then, suddenly, Declan is screaming.

'No! No way!'

He races up the gym, hurling himself at Bob, screaming.

'You're lying. You're lying.'

They collapse on the floor together. 'You're lying.'

The next thing he knows, they are sitting on the floor. Bob Fitzsimons is holding him in a bear hug with one arm; the other is pulling Declan's head onto his shoulder as he cries.

'I'm not lying, Dec. I wish I was, but I'm not. Doc's dead.'

As he says it, his whole body convulses with a sob.

'He's dead, Dec. Dead.'

6

Declan slipped into the classroom. Conor Meade — better-looking than his big brother, but just as arrogant — was making some point about the forty-eight illegal immigrants who'd recently suffocated to death as they were being smuggled into England. He looked at Declan and sighed dismissively at the interruption.

Declan looked at the teacher.

'Sorry I'm late. I was with Mr Fitzsimons.'

Miss O'Toole just nodded, and Declan made his way to the back of the class.

Before the camp, he'd been in sixth year. His future had been neatly mapped out. He'd finish school in June, spend the summer working in the bar that his brother Tony managed; then, come the autumn, he'd be heading for Texas on a basketball scholarship to study finance and marketing. All his school subject options had been geared toward that.

Since the camp, that had changed. He had no interest in finance and marketing. He had a new ambition: he wanted to qualify as a teacher, or something in development work, and go back to Nepal. His old subjects wouldn't fit either course. So he'd gone back to fifth year to start the two-year course from scratch. He could have gone to one of the 'cram colleges' and done the course in one year, but his parents couldn't afford it. Mary O'Dwyer had offered to pay for him, but he'd refused. He wanted to do it on his own. So he was back in school. Even if it held bad memories, he was familiar with it and it was free.

He listened to Conor for a few more seconds.

'I'm sorry they died and all, but it was their own choice. No one said they had to go to England. Most of them are just scroungers.'

Declan leaned forward, rested his forehead on his right hand and placed his left hand on his chest. Under his shirt he could feel the outline of the small pouch.

He wondered what Conor would make of the sign at the entrance to the camp.

'Bhutan is our homeland. We had been there for genera-tions. We had land and houses to live in. We were productive farmers, self-reliant and peace-loving people. We want to go back to our home early. This is a plea to our well-wishers to send us back with dignity, safety, security and assurance of our human rights, so the money you are spending on us can be saved for future calamities or spared for other destitute people in the world. — Bhutanese Refugees.'

It hadn't meant much to Declan the first time he'd seen it — just words and an expression of hope — but after ten months in the camp he knew exactly what it meant. The words hadn't been chosen by accident. It was a clear message: people like Kumar and the others weren't interested in charity. Kumar hadn't left his studies in California, gone back to Bhutan and joined the protest movement just to sit in a camp in Nepal and receive handouts. The refugees wanted justice.

'Can you ever really get justice?' he'd asked Kumar one night, as they were playing one-on-one on the basketball court at the edge of the camp.

'Why do you sound so sceptical?' Kumar had replied without breaking his stride.

'I was thinking of some of the stories I've heard here. Like Dil Maya. You know how she had that baby? When her husband was in jail, she was raped by Drukpa soldiers. Now her husband is in India and doesn't want anything to do with her. And when Ashok's wife was reclassified as a non-national and given two days to leave Bhutan, she had some sort of a mental breakdown and killed herself. What could count as justice for them?'

'The only justice they can get now is to have the wrong that was done to them recognised, and that won't happen until we're allowed home and get our rights and our property back. That's justice.'

'Yeah, I guess it is,' Declan had said uncertainly....

'Scroungers?' he asked angrily, under his breath.

'Declan?'

Declan jumped and glanced up. Miss O'Toole was looking at him.

'Sorry, Miss?'

'You had something to say?'

'Sorry. I was thinking out loud.'

'Prat,' laughed Conor Meade. One or two of the others sniggered too. Declan let it go.

'OK, then, Conor,' said Miss O'Toole. 'I take it that your point is that, because we didn't have an empire, we have no responsibility to the refugees? Is that correct?'

'Yes. I mean, we never invaded Asia or Africa. Britain, France and the other European powers did. So let them take the refugees in. They're not our responsibility.'

'And anyway,' added Sarah, beside him, 'refugees are spongers. They come here, live off the dole, have loads of kids to get money, and take our jobs and our houses. And with the number of kids they're having, there'll soon be more of them than there are us.'

Declan couldn't help it. He laughed out loud.

Conor and Sarah glared at him. Conor whispered, 'Weirdo,' loud enough for everyone to hear.

'Declan. You find that amusing?' asked Miss O'Toole.

'Sorry. I didn't mean to laugh out loud.'

He was going to leave it at that, but he saw them begin to snigger.

'Actually, Miss,' he said firmly, 'I don't find it amusing. More like ludicrous.'

Sarah flushed with embarrassment. *Fine,* thought Declan; *let's see how the bitch likes it when someone does to her what she did to Laura.*

'It's just that the rubbish they're spouting is exactly what people in England used to say about the Irish over there. My dad worked there for a while, years ago, and he remembers seeing signs that said, "No blacks. No dogs. No Irish."'

'So he shared a kennel with a Jamaican called Kelly,' shouted someone from Declan's left. Half the class, including Declan, laughed.

'Sorry, Miss,' apologised a kid with a mouthful of braces. His name was David Coyle, but because of the braces most people just called him Gnasher. 'I couldn't resist that. But Declan's right: exactly the same was said about us. And when you look at the number of us paddies who went to Britain, America and Australia as economic refugees, it's sickening hypocrisy for us to object to repaying the favour we owe the world. Wouldn't you agree?'

He nodded to Declan, giving the conversation back to him.

'Yes, I would,' Declan said. 'I doubt if there's anyone in this room who hasn't had someone in their family who had to emigrate. And I think that sort of cant is just ill-informed rubbish trotted out by people who're too lazy to find out the facts.'

Miss O'Toole looked at him with surprise, and Declan realised that he hadn't been just making a point. He had deliberately chosen words that would humiliate Conor and Sarah. He was attacking Conor to get at his brother.

A real Jason Meade tactic.

'I'm sorry. That's unfair,' he apologised. But it felt good to have hit back, at least a little.

'You both made some good points, you and David,' replied Miss O'Toole, 'and they're certainly worth explo —'

Her words were cut short by the bell, which was followed almost immediately by the noise of chairs being dragged back and people clattering for the door.

'Tag-team debating there, sunshine,' said Gnasher on the way out. 'We must try it again sometime.'

'Deffo,' said Declan.

'But one word of warning,' said Gnasher, in a lower voice. 'Don't turn your back on Meade. You made him look like a prat in there. His family aren't allowed to lose. Their old man's got that drummed into them. So he'll try and get you back somehow.'

Declan nodded, and Gnasher walked on ahead of him.

'They aren't allowed to lose.' Almost the same words Doc had used the night the scholarship had been announced: 'Meades aren't allowed to lose.'

That's what really made him hate me, Declan thought as he walked along. *The bloody scholarship.*

❑

Declan hadn't expected to win it. As far as he was concerned, he wasn't eligible; and anyway, he didn't know if *anyone* would be offered one.

It was Doc who'd set up the link. He'd left school and gone to study medicine at UCD. He'd made the college basketball team immediately, and that was where he'd met Dr Hugh O'Sullivan. O'Sullivan was a visiting lecturer from the University of Houston, Texas, where, in addition to teaching a course on Irish-Hispanic relations, he was an administrator for the University's basketball scholarship scheme. As an Irish-American, he was keen to set up a link between UHT and some Irish schools. So Doc had persuaded him to come to see a few of the old school games. He'd been impressed and had persuaded senior scouts from the University's basketball scholarship programme to come over.

Declan hadn't given it much thought after that. He was too young, only in fifth year — he wouldn't even have been that if he hadn't started school a year early and skipped Transition Year. If a scholarship was going to be offered to anyone, he guessed it would probably be Meade. He was the senior player and could be brilliant; he was inconsistent and selfish, but on his night he could be pure magic, winning games practically on his own.

Meade had obviously assumed the same thing. When Bob Fitzsimons announced that the scholarship had been offered to Declan and would be held over until he'd completed sixth year, Meade just glared at him and stormed off. Later, Declan had heard him screaming at Doc.

'You swung that for your little bum-boy, you poof! I'll get fucking even with you if it's the last thing I do.'

'It was nothing to do with me, Jase,' Doc had tried to answer, but Meade hadn't wanted to listen.

'This isn't over yet, faggot.'

That was when Doc had come back to look for Declan.

'Try and keep clear of Jason for a while. He's really steamed up about that scholarship. His old man will go mad. Meades aren't allowed to lose. He'll try to get even somehow.'

❑

He did that all right, pal.

7

It was Friday afternoon, last period, art class. Declan looked at the mass of wire on the desk in front of him. It was supposed to be his three-dimensional project. When it was finished, it would show Guru Rimpochet riding on a tiger to fight the evil spirits standing in the way of the spread of Buddhism in Bhutan. It was a story Kumar had told him one night as they sat in his hut.

'And do you know what's in the place where the battle is supposed to have happened?' he'd asked.

Declan shook his head.

'The Tiger's Lair temple. It's on the side of a cliff, hundreds of feet in the air. It just seems to hang onto the rock as if it's been stuck there with glue. Someday, when I'm back in Bhutan and you come to visit, we'll go there.'

Declan loved the image of the temple hanging off the cliff, and the image of the guru riding the tiger. He'd spent hours in the camp trying to sketch them. He'd never seen the temple, but anyone who saw his drawing thought he'd captured it well, and they'd all loved his sketch of the guru and the tiger.

'Maybe someday when you're a famous artist you'll

come and sketch us all,' someone had suggested. He'd like that, but not in the camps. In Bhutan.

He squinted at the wire, bending pieces here and there. Sculpting wasn't his strong point, but it wasn't too bad.

'Look who's behind you,' Gnasher whispered, walking past to throw something in the bin. Declan turned around. Laura Byrne was frowning in concentration as she leaned over her art project. He hadn't seen her in any of the morning classes or heard her come into the art room.

Gnasher walked back and stood beside him. 'Either you do it or I'll do it for you,' he whispered softly.

'Do what?' asked Declan in surprise.

'Gimme a break,' replied Gnasher. 'You know you want to talk to her.'

Declan just stared at him.

'The thirty-five quid and the T-shirt, remember?' smiled Gnasher, winking.

Declan knew exactly what he was talking about.

'So either you go over and do it now, or I'll tell her you fancy her.' Before Declan could respond, Gnasher headed towards Laura. He stopped, looked back and raised his arms in a gesture that meant, 'Do I do it or do you?'

Declan felt a rising sense of panic. He couldn't talk to Laura. He just had to keep his head down and get through 'til June. Friends would just complicate things. And what if he did get close and she found out what had happened — what then?

But he knew only one part of him was thinking like that, the rational side. There was another part of him that really wanted to talk to her. It was the part that was tired of being lonely. The part that had already made him break his own rules for her once.

❑

It was when he heard she'd been rushed to hospital with the asthma attack. All his own fears had seemed to fade away, and he'd gone to visit her.

She'd been asleep when he got there. So he'd just stood beside her bed, watching her, not sure what to do.

He'd never been that close to her before. The previous day in class she'd looked unwell, and he'd leaned at her shoulder, asking, 'You OK?' She hadn't replied. She'd just nodded.

But that was different. This was the first time he'd been close to her — alone. Funny, the things about her he hadn't noticed before.

She had tiny freckles across the bridge of her nose and there was a small mole on the nape of her neck. And her ear was pierced twice. In school, she wore her long, dark, wavy hair down over her shoulders, covering her ears. But as she slept, lying on her left side, her hair had fallen behind her head and he could see the small silver stud on the lobe and the tiny coloured butterfly almost on the top of her ear.

For a minute the sight of the butterflies had taken him back to the camp; then she'd murmured in her sleep and he'd come back to her.

He wondered if this was how Prince Charming felt looking down at Sleeping Beauty. He liked that idea. Maybe if he kissed her she would wake up and they could ride off together into the great Happy Ever After.... But he didn't kiss her. He didn't even move. He just sat there watching her sleep.

He hadn't thought it would be like this. He'd played out dozens of scenarios, on the bus journey and the walk up the hospital corridors, but none of them included her being asleep....

Declan enters the room. The girl is sitting up, maybe reading, maybe not. As he approaches her bed she looks up, pleased surprise on her face, and smiles.

'Hi,' she says.

'Hi,' he replies, returning her smile. 'I heard two of the kids in school saying you weren't well. I was on my way to town, so I thought I'd drop in and say hello.'

'That's very kind of you.' She gestures to a chair. 'Sit down.'

He sits down and they talk. They talk non-stop, hour after hour after hour, until it is time for him to go. They talk about everything — maybe even That Night. She is such a good listener, so understanding, so warm, that he feels completely at ease. He hasn't felt so at ease with anyone for more than a year. When it's time for him to leave, they exchange smiles. Then he leaves. They have each made a friend....

But it wasn't like that. She didn't wake up, and slowly being there didn't seem like such a good idea. If she woke they'd talk, and if they talked they might get close, and if they got close then one day she might find out what happened. And what then? What if she dropped him like a hot brick? What if Laura started to look at him with the same disgust and loathing that he felt for himself — what then?

Some things are even worse than being alone. So he'd left. At least, he'd started to; and then quickly he'd turned back, kissed the ends of his fingers and pressed them softly against her long hair. Then he'd turned away and slipped out, leaving a small parcel at the bottom of her bed.

It was better like that.

❑

Gnasher looked at him again and mouthed the words, 'You or me.'

Declan pointed to himself. If someone was going to do this, it might just as well be him. He put down his pliers and walked over to Laura.

She was looking at the photo of a young boy, propped against her art project. Declan stood behind her. For a second he didn't know what to say. Then he leaned slightly forward.

'A boyfriend?' he smiled. As soon he'd said it he felt stupid.

Laura looked up and smiled shyly.

'Hi,' she said. 'Thanks a million for the T-shirt. It was really sweet of you. I was going to thank you when I came in, but you looked so caught up in your sculpture that I decided I'd wait until after class.'

He nodded. No one had ever called him sweet before.

'You're better, then?' he said, stating the obvious. 'Only I heard it was a really bad asthma attack that time, and you nearly died.'

'Slight exaggeration,' she smiled. 'But it was bad. I'm OK now, though, thanks.'

There was a silence. Declan had no idea what to say next. Maybe he should just leave it at that and go.

Laura seized the initiative, and picked up the photo.

'His name is Sanjid,' she said, handing Declan the picture. 'He's six years old, and for two years he was a slave in the carpet sheds of Mirzapur, in India, but now he's in a safe place.'

'What are the carpet sheds?' asked Declan.

'They're a bloody crime,' she said seriously.

She stopped and looked at him, as if unsure whether she should carry on or not.

'Go on,' he encouraged her.

It seemed as if she'd just been waiting for someone to ask her about it. So he listened. Even after what he'd seen in the camps, he couldn't believe what she was telling him. He'd heard about child labour before, but never bonded child labour — millions of kids being forced to make carpets to pay off family debts; kids kidnapped and sold to the shed owners: kids working eighteen hours a day, every day of the year, beaten if they complained, if they made a mistake, if they worked too slowly. And it wasn't just carpets. Bonded kids were used in hundreds of industries, most of which were selling goods that were in the shops in Ireland.

The kid in the picture could have been any of the kids from the camp — any little kid Declan had ever seen in Dublin, for that matter. It made him feel sick just to think about it.

What he found amazing was that Laura wasn't just trotting out facts and figures and names as if they were something she'd picked up for a school project. When she spoke, she spoke with real passion, as angry over what happened to these kids as if they were people she knew. It was almost as if she'd been there.

'How do you know all this?' he asked.

'You know how it is when you get concerned about something; you just sort of pick up bits and pieces everywhere.'

She sat back, and he thought she looked drained by it all.

'That sort of knowledge can really overwhelm you, can't it?' he said softly.

'You've no idea how much.'

Tears started to run down her cheek.

Instinctively, Declan reached out and gently wiped her tears away with his thumb. It felt so natural, as if he'd been doing it all his life. As he looked at her big, moist brown eyes, he suddenly knew why he'd wanted to talk to her. She was lonely too.

'The question is,' he said, as the bell rang for the end of school, 'where do you go from here? Now that you have the knowledge, what do you do about it?'

Laura shrugged. 'I don't know, but I can't just go on as if I'd never heard about it all. I have to do something. Maybe I can start a letter-writing campaign in school. Maybe I could organise a fund-raiser for Mukti Ashram, or —'

'Mukti who?'

'Ashram. It's the place where SACCS brings freed child workers for rehabilitation and training. Maybe we can do a fund-raiser for them, or sponsor a freed child, or ...'

Declan smiled. 'It's not easy to decide, is it? But, hey — nothing worthwhile ever is.'

She glanced back at the photo. Declan knew he couldn't just leave it there. He couldn't just say, 'Well, thanks for sharing that with me. See you around,' and walk off. He should, but he couldn't. He'd already gone too far.

'Er — listen, would you fancy going for a coffee?' he asked awkwardly.

'Sure. I'd love to, but only if you promise to tell me about that famous missing year of yours.'

'It was only ten months, actually, but I'll tell you some of it. Deal?'

'Deal.'

'I'll just grab my bag.'

He went back to his desk and swung his bag up onto his shoulder. Gnasher was trying to feign disinterest, but Declan knew he was watching him; so he slipped his hand behind his back and gave Gnasher a thumbs-up sign. Then he went back to Laura.

'Ready?'

'Sure.'

They walked towards the door.

'Hey, Laura!'

They turned around. Gnasher was sitting on the edge of his desk, fiddling with his project.

'Don't strain your neck looking up at that big sap,' he grinned.

'Don't worry, Dave, I won't. But thanks for the advice.'

'Thanks, pal,' said Declan.

They stepped out into the corridor and closed the door behind them. Laura looked up at him.

'You used to play basketball, didn't you?'

'What gave you the clue, my height?' he laughed.

'No, I used to see you coming into your practice just as we were leaving badminton, and it was all over school about you getting some scholarship to America. But you've given it up now, haven't you?'

Declan just nodded.

'Do you mind me asking why? Everyone says you were great.'

'I don't know about that bit. But basketball just doesn't seem the same any more. Not since ...'

He let it trail off.

'Since your friend died. What was his name — Kieran Docherty?'

'Yeah, we called him Doc,' Declan said softly. 'Since him and — well, a lot of other stuff.'

'Dare I ask?'

'Not just yet. I'll explain some of it over coffee.'

Laura smiled warmly.

'I'll hold you to that, Mr Donnelly.'

Mr Donnelly. He liked the playful humour of that.

'That's OK, Miss Byrne, and I'll honour it — but only if we trade off, because you're something of an enigma to me.'

'I don't know what that means, but it better not be bad,' she said as they reached the school gates.

'Puzzle,' Declan replied.

'Me, a puzzle?' Laura said in genuine surprise. 'I'm far from it. What you see is what you get.'

'OK, then, how about this? I saw you once with those other girls, and you were a weird mix. Them all dressed up like models, and you in combats....'

'Where was that?'

'Outside a cinema.'

'And you didn't say hello?'

'That's another story. But anyway, how come you were

hanging around with them? You don't have the same fashion sense, and from what I heard in class you don't have the same views. I wouldn't mind betting you don't even like the same music.'

'Actually, they think my taste in music is — how did Cass put it? — crap.'

'See what I mean? So how come you were hanging around with them?'

'Because I've been with them since primary. We were the Four Horsemen of the Potato Crisps, indivisible, one for all and all for one,' she laughed.

'That was the Three Musketeers,' Declan offered.

'Yeah, OK. Anyway, you get the point. They were the only pals I'd ever had. I couldn't see how I'd get on without them, even if we didn't have much in common any more.'

'And what about Conor Meade? I thought you were going out with him.'

'You must be joking!' Laura shook her head. 'He was my badminton partner, beginning, middle and end — whatever he liked to think. Anyway, enough about me. Your turn. Tell me about Declan Donnelly.'

'OK. I'm the youngest of five. My eldest brother is forty-four, and both my parents are retired. My eldest nephew is ...'

If they passed anyone else as they walked down to the café in the local shopping centre, Declan didn't notice. His complete attention was on Laura. As they walked along, trading background histories and stories about their families, he realised that he was feeling totally relaxed for the first time in nearly a year. Even with Kumar, he hadn't felt this much at ease. He knew he was taking a chance, but he wanted to do it. He was almost disappointed when they reached the café and he had to share her, even indirectly, with the other people in the room.

He sipped his coffee and looked at Sanjid's photo.

'I've seen a lot of little kids like him, boys and girls. Bhutanese refugees.'

'Where's Bhutan?' asked Laura.

Declan pulled a Biro from his blazer pocket and traced a rough map on a paper table-napkin.

'This is India, there's Nepal and there's Bhutan,' he said, pointing to the various squares. 'And here's where the refugee camps for the Bhutanese are.' He circled an area in southern Nepal. 'The people in the camps are Bhutanese Hindus, ethnic Nepalese, who were forced out of their homes and off their lands by the Bhutanese government.'

'Why?'

Declan shook his head and shrugged. 'Good question. Some people say that the government saw census figures showing that ethnic Nepalis comprised about thirty per cent of the population and their numbers were still rising, so they became concerned that their own culture would be swamped. Others say it was the monarchy trying to hold on to absolute power in the face of increasing calls for democracy. I don't really know. But whatever the reason, since 1988 more than a hundred thousand refugees have swarmed into the camps in south-eastern Nepal.'

'I've never heard anything about that,' Laura admitted.

'Don't worry, most people here haven't. A friend of mine in the camps, a Bhutanese man named Kumar, once said to me: "We're just a bunch of nobodies from Bhutan sitting here rotting, while the rest of the world ignores us. If we had oil or strategic value the West would be in here in a minute. But we have nothing. So does anybody care?"'

'How did you find out?'

Declan thought for a second. He would have liked to tell her the truth. The long version.

❑

When Bob Fitzsimons tells them about Doc's death, Declan's body and spirit seem to separate.

His body takes on a life of its own. The real Declan is on the outside, watching, listening to a voice that doesn't seem to belong to him.

He sees the body walk home from school as classes are cancelled for the day. He watches it go through some sort of routine of eating and talking. He sees it a couple of days later, on 21 December, attending the funeral mass and joining all the other members of the basketball teams to form a guard of honour. He observes it sniffling as it sees Doc's body lowered into the ground, and looks at Mr and Mrs Docherty collapsing into each other's arms. He watches it open its presents and go through the routine of Christmas Day and Stephen's Day.

Then comes 27 December, and he rejoins his body with a bang.

He has more or less convinced himself that Doc's death had nothing to do with That Night. It was an accident. His car hit a tree on the way to college. 'It happens,' he told himself. 'Even to people you know. And even if it did happen only three days later, it was still an accident, not my fault.'

But when the numbness is gone, when he is back in his body, he knows. He killed Doc, as surely as if he'd driven the car into that tree himself.

The sick, cramping knot of pain is back between his legs and in his stomach. He has to get out. He has to get away, find somewhere to scream and rage and swear and break down in tears all on his own, away from his parents and brothers and sisters and nieces and nephews and all the hugs and sympathetic pats on the shoulder. His best friend is dead, and it is his fault.

So he walks, walks without any real direction or logic. Suddenly he is in the city. As he nears Temple Bar, a thought strikes him: the river. All he has to do is walk down the steps into the cold deep water, let it close over him, and all the confusion, all the disgust, the anger and the shame will be gone for ever. It is a selfish impulse, he realises that later, but just then it seems like such a good idea. And so he walks down to the river and along the quays.

And as he passes along the quays he sees a book, lying in a basket outside a second-hand bookshop. The bright, childish drawing on the cover catches his eye. He has never heard of Bhutan, so the title, I See Bhutan In My Dreams, doesn't mean anything to him. But then he sees the drawings and reads the stories: parents tied and beaten, forced at gunpoint to sign away their homes, their houses burnt in front of them, soldiers with knives cutting naked prisoners. It turns his stomach.

Three weeks later he is in Nepal, climbing into Mary's jeep.

❑

He wanted to tell Laura all that, but he didn't. He hadn't even told Kumar. He told her the short version.

'I only found out about it last November, when I picked up a picture book done by the refugee children; but I couldn't stop thinking about it. That's why I headed off to the camp last January. I had to do something.'

'So you were in the camps? That's amazing!'

'Now you know the great secret of the missing months. You're the only one outside my family who does.'

'Thanks for telling me,' said Laura. 'I promise I won't tell anyone else.'

'I know.'

She smiled, and Declan smiled back. He could have stayed there all night, just talking, but he sensed that she wanted to leave. He looked at his watch.

'We'd better go. I'll just pay.'

Laura nodded, and Declan went up to the counter. At least he'd made a start; they'd made a start. That was the main thing.

Briefly, as he paid, he wondered again if he'd made a mistake. He'd promised himself he wouldn't get close to anyone.... As he went back to the table, Laura was looking at the photo again. She whispered something he couldn't quite catch. It sounded like 'Rosa.'

How in God's name could she be a mistake?

'What was that you were saying just now? "Rosa"? Another friend?'

Laura blushed. 'Another part of the — what was it you called me?'

'An enigma.'

'Another part of the enigma. Maybe I'll tell you some time.'

'Quite a pair of bloody mysteries, aren't we? I look forward to us getting to know more about each other, Miss Byrne.'

'So do I, Mr Donnelly,' she smiled. 'So do I.'

As they stepped out of the café, Laura looked at the sky and checked her watch. Four o'clock.

'Declan, do you do normally go home straight after school?' she asked.

'Not really. I have my dad's car today, so I'm in no rush. I just thought you might want to get home.'

'I do, today. It's just — well, I promised David and Barbara I'd do a photo shoot for them ...'

'You're a photographer too! My God, I am impressed, Miss Byrne.'

Laura smiled. 'Yeah. It's sort of an obsession of mine. Anyway, they're starting a band and I promised to do some photos, and I wanted to check out spots in the park. It's a handy location. I'm going to my aunt's in Kilkenny for the weekend, but I thought I might do it Monday, after school. I don't really fancy heading down there on my own. I was just wondering, would you come with me?'

Declan was delighted with the invitation. She obviously felt as relaxed in his company as he did in hers.

'Sure, no problem.'

'See you Monday, then,' Laura said.

She started to walk away. Declan just watched her go. Then she turned back and smiled.

'And, Declan?'

'Yes?'

'Thanks.'

'For what?'

'For listening.'

He smiled and waved. Then she walked on and Declan turned, heading back up towards the school to collect his father's car.

You are breaking your rules, he warned himself. *If things go wrong, you'll have no one else to blame.*

I'll take that risk, he thought.

For a few moments he'd felt normal. He wanted to jump for joy. He wanted to go on feeling like that.

8

'Did you see him, did ya? Did ya? Jackie just sort of dropped his left shoulder, brought all his weight onto his left foot, then raised his right leg and snapped it out, one, two, three times, and caught each one of them just under the eye. Did you *see* it, did ya?'

Declan laughed as Darragh spun around, giving his impression of the Jackie Chan film they'd just seen.

'Of course we saw it, you prat,' said Jonathan. 'We were watching the same film.'

'Yeah, but did you really *see* it?' asked Darragh again.

Declan loved the banter between the two of them. He could listen to it all night.

It was Friday night. They were standing outside the cinema in the shopping centre, waiting for Macker to emerge so they could decide where to go next.

It was the first time he'd been out with them since he'd been home. Every week Darragh had asked him, and every week he'd found some excuse to say no. But tonight he'd phoned Darragh and asked if they could all go out. He had Laura Byrne to thank for that. Talking to her, that afternoon, had made him think that maybe he could take a few chances — not with everyone, but with a few special people, like her and Darragh and the boys. He was tired of being on his own.

He watched them circling each other. Jonathan adopted some pretend karate pose and said in his best Chinese-villain accent, 'You come to avenge your father. But I tell you, your father betrayed us, and the betrayal of the clan must be avenged on all of his family. So now you die!'

Darragh jumped in front of Declan, pushing him backwards.

'You will not take my uncle, old man!' He glared at Jonathan. 'I will protect my family to the death.'

God, I've missed all this, Declan thought.

Macker came skipping down the steps of the cinema, eating a hot dog. He looked from Darragh to Jonathan and shook his head. Then he grabbed Declan by the shoulder and led him towards the exit doors of the shopping centre.

'Tell me, Declan, how did a sound man like you ever end up with a prat like that for a nephew?'

'You'll have to ask our Jamesie,' replied Declan. 'Nothing to do with me.'

Macker turned back. The other two were still circling each other, but a security man was beginning to notice their display and move towards them.

'Oi! You! Donnelly!' Macker shouted at Darragh. 'Grow up and act your age. You're embarrassing your old uncle here.'

People were looking at them. Declan felt himself blush.

'Thanks for being so discreet, Macker,' he said. 'And, by the way, that prat is three months older than me.'

'Some weird family you got there, boy,' replied Macker in his best western drawl. He took a bite of his hot dog, put it in the bin and pulled on his ski hat.

'So what's happening now? We going to —'

He didn't get the chance to finish the sentence. There was

a rush of feet behind him, a hand grabbed his hat, and Darragh and Jonathan rushed past him, through the doors and across the car park.

'Creeps!' Macker called, racing after them.

Declan stopped in front of the doors of the shopping mall, watching them go. He needed more of this. Before he went to the camps, they'd done this once a week. The others weren't his pals, they were Darragh's, but they'd always included him as part of the group. Maybe they could start up the once-a-week outing again, and maybe if things worked out with Laura she could become part of the group, and maybe even Gnasher — he seemed OK.

It felt good to be back, to be normal.

The door behind him opened, hitting him in the back.

'Sorry,' he began, turning around. He stopped. Jason Meade was grinning; Cahill and O'Connor were standing behind him.

'Look who's here. Declan. No little boys to hang around with, Dec?'

'Grow up, prats,' said Declan turning to leave. He didn't want to see them, not now.

Meade grabbed his arm. 'That's not very respectful, is it now, Deckie?'

Declan turned. Inside he was quaking, but he tried not to show it. He'd have to brazen this out. He forced himself to look at Meade, pretending he was staring right through him.

'If you want to keep that hand, move it, *now*,' he said firmly, praying his voice wouldn't tremble and give him away.

'Ooh! We're scared,' said Cahill, pretending to tremble.

Declan ignored him. He just continued to glare through Meade without really seeing him. He felt Meade's grip loosen.

'Dec! Hey, Dec!'

Declan turned around. Darragh, Jonathan and Macker were coming across the car park.

'Some other time,' said Meade. 'We'll leave you with your boyfriends.' He turned and walked off towards the cinema.

Declan leaned against the door. He was shaking with fear; he wanted to crawl away and cry. All the good feelings were gone. Suddenly, he felt totally deflated.

Bastards! he screamed silently. *They couldn't even give me tonight.*

'What's that all about?' asked Darragh, nodding after Meade.

'Nothing,' said Declan, controlling his voice. 'He was just letting off hot air.' He laughed, trying to make the remark sound off-hand.

'Pity. I'm just dying for an excuse to kick that fucker's teeth down his throat. He better not come back to our school for any basketball matches or he's a dead man.'

'Why?' asked Declan.

'He elbowed one of our team in the eye.'

'That can happen,' said Declan, trying to sound normal.

'Not four times,' said Jonathan. 'And all when the ref wasn't in a position to see.'

'He's a sneaky little thug,' added Macker. 'We're just dying for a reason to flatten him.'

Declan was very tempted to give them one, but he didn't. He just wanted to get home.

9

Declan sat down beside Doc's grave. He opened the can of Lucozade and raised it to his lips.

'Cheers.'

He took a long drink.

It was Saturday morning. He hadn't intended to come today, but he needed to talk to someone. Laura, the boys — they had made him feel good, normal again. But seeing Meade had destroyed all that. He couldn't ever really be like everyone else. The first night and That Night would always be there, getting in the way.

He wasn't even sure what to do about Laura now. All the other stuff would always be waiting in the wings to get in the way — and then there were Meade and friends. If Declan was with Laura and ran into them, they'd humiliate him somehow. How would Laura react to that? How would he?

Maybe he should just ignore her and go back to being on his own. That would be the safest thing to do, but he didn't want to. His mind was spinning.

'There's this girl, Doc....'

He closed his eyes, remembering how they'd sat in the café talking. How he'd loved watching her smile, the way she called him 'Mr Donnelly', the way her eyes had sparkled with life when she spoke about the carpet kids. It had been a long time since he'd felt like that....

'So what do you reckon, Doc?' he asked eventually, without opening his eyes. 'Do I play it safe and keep away from her, or do I run the risk and keep talking to her?'

'Personally, chum, I'd talk to her. If you mean Laura.'

Declan jumped and opened his eyes.

Gnasher was standing just a few feet away.

'Sorry, Dec. I didn't mean to startle you,' he said uncomfortably. Declan didn't reply.

'I had to bring Sharon to see Nan's grave,' he continued. He nodded at somewhere behind Declan. Declan turned around; a young Down's Syndrome girl was standing a few rows away. She smiled at him and waved. He waved back.

'I just saw you sitting there and thought I'd say hi. I shouldn't have intruded.'

Declan still didn't reply; he was still too caught up in his own thoughts. Gnasher turned and started to walk away.

What the hell am I doing? thought Declan suddenly, snapping out of his self-obsession.

'David!' he called.

Gnasher turned around in surprise; then he pretended to look around to see who was being called, and pointed to himself in mock shock, mouthing 'Me?'

Declan smiled and nodded. He pushed himself up.

'I thought you knew by now,' said Gnasher. 'The only people who call me David are teachers, my parents, Sharon, Laura Byrne and the police. Everyone else calls me Gnasher.'

'OK, Gnasher.'

'Much better.'

'Listen, I'm sorry. I wasn't being ignorant to you just then.' Declan paused, half-expecting Gnasher to offer the normal denial or reassurance. He didn't.

'It's just — you sort of startled me, and it took me a few seconds to get my thoughts back together. I was off somewhere else.'

'Yeah. I noticed.'

Gnasher looked at the grave. 'He seemed like an OK bloke,' he offered. 'I didn't really know him. I just saw him around the area and at school. Shaz knew him, though,' he said, nodding at his sister. 'They were in playschool together.'

Declan looked surprised.

'Yeah, hard to imagine her in with ordinary kids, isn't it?'

'I didn't mean that — I —'

'It's OK. I know you didn't mean anything by it. No, they were always fond of each other, him and Sharon.'

'He was a good kid,' said Declan.

'Only the good die young,' smiled Gnasher. 'Me nan always used to say that. So I reckon I'm safe till about three hundred.'

Declan laughed.

'David! David! I've finished all my prayers,' shouted Sharon excitedly. 'Shall I start again or are we going?'

'No, don't,' Gnasher shouted back urgently. He smiled at Declan. 'If I don't stop her she'd keep us here all day, praying and singing hymns. She knows bloody hundreds of them. I'd better get her out while I still have half a chance. See you around.'

He walked off towards Sharon.

'Da ... Gnasher,' Declan called after him. 'Do you want a lift? I've got my dad's car.'

'What do you reckon, Shaz? Shall we go on the bus or take a ride in the car?'

Sharon hooded her eyes, screwed up her mouth and rubbed her chin with her finger and thumb as if she was giving it serious thought.

'Now don't take all day, Shaz, or Declan will go without us.'

Sharon bit her thumb for a second. Then she pulled it out of her mouth and gave a broad smile that almost made her eyes disappear.

'We'll go by car,' she announced.

'Good,' said Gnasher. He took her hand. Then he turned to Declan.

'Lead on, Macduff.'

'That's a funny name,' said Sharon. 'Macduff.'

'No, it's not his ...' began Gnasher; then he had another idea. 'It's just his nickname. Just like yours is Stinky!'

'No it's not,' laughed Sharon, hitting him. 'My nickname's Lotus Blossom. You said you call me that 'cause I look Chinese.'

'Oh, that's right,' laughed Gnasher. 'I forgot — Stinky.'

Sharon hit him again. Then she looked at Declan and winked.

'Lead on, Macduff.'

'Certainly, Madam.' Declan bowed. Then he looked towards Doc's grave.

See you soon, Doc. Wish me luck.

As he turned to walk away, he was surprised to find Sharon grabbing his other hand.

'Doc's gone away,' she said.

'He has,' Declan nodded.

'He went away after the bad boys called him names. They won't call him names any more,' she told him.

Gnasher and Declan looked at each other in surprise.

'What bad boys ?' asked Gnasher. 'When?'

'Before he went away, silly, the Saturday.'

'What did they say? Who were they?'

'I promised I wouldn't tell,' she grinned. 'They were just bad boys.'

'Who, Sharon?' Declan asked.

She clamped her mouth tightly shut and shook her head.

'Who —' he began.

'No point,' shrugged Gnasher. 'When she clams up like that, she won't say a word about it.'

Declan looked at Sharon and smiled. 'Please?'

She just shook her head and closed her eyes.

'Stubborn old biddy,' grinned Gnasher.

Sharon laughed and punched him on the arm. 'And you're old smelly-socks,' she laughed.

Declan felt a sickening pain in his stomach. It rose slowly into his throat. He winced and leaned breathlessly against the car.

He was certain Sharon meant Meade and friends. *They couldn't leave it at what they'd done, could they? They probably saw him on the street and couldn't resist taunting him about it....*

'You OK?' asked Gnasher, putting his hand on Declan's shoulder.

'Yeah, fine. It'll pass in a minute. Just a touch of stomach cramp. I get it every now and again,' Declan replied, not quite lying.

'Fair enough,' replied Gnasher, but Declan could sense he didn't believe him.

For most of the three-mile journey back to Gnasher's house, Declan didn't open his mouth except to answer any questions Gnasher or Sharon asked. His replies were mono-syllabic. Gnasher didn't notice; Sharon's non-stop chatter and excitement, as she pointed out everything they passed, more than made up for Declan's lack of conversation.

Declan followed Gnasher's directions, and they pulled up at a neat little semi-detached house in the private housing estate near the school.

'Welcome to Coyle Mansions,' announced Gnasher. 'Would you like to come in for a cuppa?'

Declan thought about it for a second. Would that be a step too far too soon? But it could be just noncommittal polite conversation....

'Sure, that'd be nice.'

As soon as they were in the house Sharon raced into the kitchen, took off her coat and started working on a jigsaw puzzle that lay half-completed on the kitchen table.

'That's her gone for the next few hours,' said Gnasher.

He pushed the door to the lounge and peeped in.

'Hi, Mam, we're back.'

A blonde woman who didn't look old enough to be his mother looked up from behind a pile of paperwork on the coffee table. 'Oh, hi, love.'

She looked at Declan and smiled.

'This is Declan, Mam,' said Gnasher.

Declan walked forward and shook her hand. It felt soft and smooth.

'Nice to meet you, Declan. You aren't from the area, are you?'

'No, I live up near the shopping centre.'

'We're in the same class,' said Gnasher. 'I've just invited him back for a cuppa.'

'Fine. Just this once I'll make it and bring it up to you, but don't expect this treatment all the time.'

'As if,' laughed Gnasher.

Gnasher led the way upstairs to his bedroom. A three-tiered rack of keyboards dominated the room.

'Yours?'

Gnasher nodded.

'Well, sort of mine and my dad's. He played in the tail end of the showband era. He's good, too, but he doesn't play much now — only at the odd party or maybe the odd re-union. But these things helped him keep body and soul together when his company went under.'

'Oh.'

'I'll tell you about it sometime.' He looked at Declan, who'd seated himself on a chair by the desk.

'Will you answer me something? You don't have to —

you can tell me to sod off and mind my own business if you like; but what would stop you talking to Laura, now that you've started?'

'Long story, and I don't know if I can go into it right now, if that's OK.'

'Sure, whatever you say.'

The awkward silence that followed was broken by the arrival of Gnasher's mother with coffee and biscuits.

'I'll keep my nose out of it after this,' said Gnasher, once she'd gone, 'but you really should talk to Laura. She needs decent friends. You've seen those prats she was hanging around with. They're just not her sort of people. She needs someone who doesn't think the world stops at the bounds of their own ego.'

'And how do you know I don't?'

'I heard you destroy Meade and Braindead's efforts at debate, remember?'

Declan smiled. 'They were getting on my nerves, reducing the whole thing to tabloid headlines, when it's so much more complex. Anyway, you were just as vociferous as me.'

'See, that's the sort of thing I mean,' said Gnasher, laughing. 'Those prats couldn't even use words like complex or vociferous. They think marmalade and corrugated are big words.'

It was Declan's turn to laugh.

'It wasn't just what you said, though,' Gnasher continued. 'It was the fact that you really seemed to care. That's why I think Laura needs a friend like you: she's got all this stuff she really cares about too, but those prats just treat her like a joke. After what I've noticed over the last couple of weeks, though, I don't think she'll be hanging around with them again. They never even bothered their arses to go and see her in hospital. Some friends, huh? She needs a pal like you.'

'There you go again. You don't even know me.'

'OK, let's see about that. You care enough about your old mate to visit him at least once a week since you got back from wherever you were.'

Declan looked surprised.

'It's not hard to figure it out. We're there every weekend, and Sharon always visits Doc as well; and there's always an old Lucozade can on the grave. And what did you put there today?'

'A half-empty can of Lucozade.'

'So let's chalk that down: loyalty to a mate and caring. And you've got this thing about Bhutan.'

Declan was even more surprised. 'How —'

Gnasher laughed. 'We're in the same art class, remember? When Miss Farrell asked us to choose a topic, you chose old Guru Thingy riding his elephant into battle.'

'It's Rimpochet and it's a tiger.'

'You said it was an old Bhutanese legend. And then, that time in the library, when we were collecting for Laura's thing for whatever it was and you offered us the thirty-five quid, you were on the Internet reading reports about the Bhutanese refugee crisis.'

'How —'

'I looked over your shoulder when I walked past, and because I'd never heard about Bhutan till then, I checked it out in Amnesty. So, see, you care about things like that. Just like Laura.'

'You're some bloody cookie, do you know that?'

'And I'll tell you something else,' continued Gnasher. 'You hate Conor Meade's big brother, what's his face.'

'Jason. How do you work that one out?'

'The way you went for Conor and Sarah the other day. You acted like they were old enemies; and, prats though they are, you don't know them that well. But you play basketball, and I know Jason is always throwing his weight around with the younger kids up there. They hate the bastard, they really do. You should hear them talking about him.'

He stretched back on the chair and looked at Declan.

'They all loved you and Doc, though. They said you made every one of them feel like he was Michael Jordan.'

'How —'

'You know Tommy Carolan?'

'Tommy? Little red-haired Tommy with freckles and a big grin, about four feet nothing?'

'Yeah, that's him.'

'You bet I know him.'

'He's Kelz's little brother.'

'Who?'

'Kelz. Barbara Carolan, my girlfriend. Anyway, Tommy thinks you and Doc were the greatest things since sliced bread.'

Declan looked away.

'Do you know what he does to get back at Meade and his two wanker mates, Cahill and O'Connor?' said Gnasher, laughing.

'What?'

'You know those screw-top sports bottles that Meade and his poser mates carry? Filled with glucose drinks?'

'Yeah?'

'Tommy and his mates take a sip of the drink and then piss into what's left to fill it up again. Then they watch Meade and his buddies drink it.'

Declan burst out laughing. It was virtually the first time he'd laughed since he came home.

'Fantastic!'

The sudden ringing of the telephone interrupted the laughter. Gnasher picked it up.

Declan listened to the one-sided conversation.

'Yeah, I did.... You did? That's great.... Friday? Sure, no problem. Just the two of us.... Yeah.... Fine. Thanks.'

Gnasher put the phone down and beamed. 'Wait till she hears this!' He immediately picked up the phone again and dialled. 'Just ringing Kelz.'

'Kelz? It's me. Guess what? The guy from Sound Box was on. He liked our demo tape, and he offered us a spot on their showcase night on Friday.... Yeah, I know! I said we'd do it. OK? ... Good. Listen, come over in about half an hour and we'll go through a couple of numbers.... Yeah, me too. See you then.'

As Gnasher talked, Declan looked around the room. The bookshelves caught his eye.

On one shelf, the complete Steinbeck collection was sandwiched in between Terry Pratchett and James Watson. Below them, Sylvia Plath, Ted Hughes, Paula Meehan and Rita Anne Higgins were joined by the complete Winnie-the-Pooh, all seven volumes of the Chronicles of Narnia, Lord of the Rings, two books by John Pilger and several books on mythology.

'I suppose you gathered that we've got a chance to play at Sound Box next week,' said Gnasher, beaming. 'I dropped them a demo tape we made, and the guy liked it.'

'"We" being who, exactly?'

'Me and Kelz. We call ourselves Don't Bite The Donkey Mon.'

'What?'

'Yeah. Great, ain't it? Like to hear our tape? We recorded it here and mastered it on the computer.'

Before Declan could reply, Gnasher had pushed a tape into his stereo and pressed play.

The sound of a drum — Declan guessed it was a snare drum — came floating across the room. Then came a girl's voice. At first it sounded miles away, but gradually it came closer and closer, while synthesised music and an acoustic guitar played softly underneath. The voice was amazingly clear, and the diction was perfect.

'Boy soldier,
Boy soldier,
They put a gun into your hand,
You'll fill a grave as good as any man,
Boy soldier.

Boy soldier,
Boy soldier,
They don't care about your age,
You can shoot a gun and throw a hand grenade,
Boy soldier.

And they steal you, beat you, scare you, treat you
As some object to stop a knife
Or a bullet or a bomb or a mortar shell, and boy soldier,
They deprive you of your right
To childhood.
Boy soldier,
Boy soldier,
And you're not yet quite a teen,
The world won't stop this obscene
Use of you,
Boy soldier....'

Then the whole thing was repeated, fading to the sound of gunfire, groans and someone repeating statistics on the number of children forced into war in a slow, low, emotionless voice.

'Well, what do you think?' asked Gnasher.

'Incredible. Sounds so professional. Where did you get the song?'

'I wrote it.'

'Really?'

'Yeah.'

'Bloody amazing.'

'She's got some voice, hasn't she?'

'Unbelievable. And that's Kelz?'

'Yeah!'

'She sounds like — I don't know — a more powerful Sinéad O'Connor, or Dolores Keane without the accent. I'll have to see you guys sometime.'

'Come this Friday.'

'Yeah. I just might. '

'And maybe you could ask Laura to come.'

Declan laughed; even for Gnasher, the set-up was pretty obvious. 'I'd better go. You've got Barbara —'

'Kelz.'

'Kelz coming over. And I have to go anyway. Thanks for ... Well, you know.'

'Yeah.'

They headed downstairs, and Declan popped his head around the lounge door. 'Bye, Mrs Coyle. Nice meeting you.'

'Same here, Declan. Do come again.'

He nodded.

In the kitchen, Sharon was still busy with her jigsaw.

'Bye, Sharon.'

'Bye, Macduff,' she replied without looking up.

'See you on Monday,' Declan said to Gnasher, in the doorway.

'Sure thing.'

As Declan got into the car, Kelz turned in to the Coyles' garden. She smiled at Declan and put her arm around Gnasher. He watched them in his wing mirror.

God, how he envied them their closeness.

10

Declan seemed to spend all of Monday waiting for the last bell. Their usual Monday art class had been cancelled for some reason, and they'd all been sent to other options, so he'd only seen Laura once, in the corridor. She'd turned around, noticed him and smiled. It made him feel good. She really could be a friend, if he let her. And he'd decided he would.

He hadn't seen Tommy, which surprised him, because on the way to school he'd seen him hanging around near the building site.

At three-thirty the bell finally rang. Declan almost raced to the gate. Laura was waiting for him.

'Thanks for remembering,' she smiled.

'As if I'd forget.'

'Declan! Declan!' Tommy was rushing down the road. He nodded to Laura and turned straight to Declan.

'Have you decided yet?' he asked, grinning.

'No. But I'm thinking about it.'

'Great,' grinned Tommy. 'I'd better go before any of the teachers see me.'

And he rushed back up the road, dragging his school-bag behind him.

Declan watched him go and shook his head. 'He's persistent, I'll give him that.'

'What was that all about?' asked Laura.

'He wants me to start coaching the second-years again.'

'And will you?'

'I honestly don't know. There are a couple of things to consider.'

'Dare I ask?'

'Not just yet.'

'Fair enough.'

'You don't mind me not telling you?'

'No, honest,' Laura said, smiling. 'Let's make it a rule that we only tell each other what we're comfortable with. That way there's no pressure.'

'Agreed, Miss Byrne.'

They crossed the road into the park, talking about nothing in particular. Declan felt as if he'd known her for years rather than just a couple of days. She didn't seem to have any pretensions, 'notions about herself', as his mother might say. He was pretty certain that with Laura Byrne it was a case of 'what you see is what you get'.

They entered the park, and Laura stopped talking. She opened her bag, pulled out her camera and lifted it to her eye, checking through the viewfinder.

'Just framing to get an impression of what it'll look like,' she informed Declan. He nodded.

They walked beyond the ponds and around the playing fields, over the ornamental bridge and towards the children's playground, then back across the footbridge and towards the artificial lakes. Every now and then they would meet other kids, a lot of them couples holding hands or with their arms wrapped around each other. Some nodded, some said 'Hi,' and some just smiled. Declan and Laura nodded back. It was only when Declan heard a fourth-year talking to his girlfriend that he realised why people were being so friendly.

'I never knew they were going out,' the boy said.

Declan wanted to turn around and say, 'No, we're just here together walking.' If Laura had heard the comment he probably would have. But she was too busy framing locations even to notice, so he let it go. Then he realised that, mistake or not, he liked the idea that people might think he and Laura were an item. It gave him a warm glow. At least they weren't looking at him as some sort of freak.

As they reached the ornamental ponds, he heard someone calling, 'Macduff!' He turned around. Gnasher and Sharon were emerging from behind one of the rocks that surrounded the second lake. Sharon was clutching something in her hand.

'Macduff, Macduff,' she called, running up to Declan. 'Look what I've got!' She opened her palm to show a handful of tiny stones.

'These are for my collection.' Then she saw Laura. 'Look, Laura. I've got loads of new stones. David helped me find them.'

'Wow! They're really pretty, Sharon. Let's have a closer look.' Laura picked the stones up one by one and looked at them.

'This is what we do, twice a year,' said Gnasher, smiling. 'In spring we have to pick the "fresh" stones, and in autumn or winter we have to pick the "old" stones. It sort of started as a joke, when we were kids. Fresh flowers grew in the spring, conkers fell off the trees in autumn, so Sharon decided the same thing happened to stones. I'm not sure if she actually believes it or not, but it's our little ritual.'

'Ritual's important,' Declan replied, thinking of himself and Doc and the Lucozade ritual. 'It's what makes a relationship special.'

'Talking of which,' said Gnasher, letting Laura and Sharon walk slightly ahead, 'I'm glad to see you decided to keep talking to our mutual friend.'

'So am I.'

'And how's it going?'

'You mean all thirty minutes or so of it?'

'I can't help it,' Gnasher grinned. 'I'm an incurable romantic.'

Declan was about to reply when Laura turned around. 'Was Declan telling you, we've been out spotting locations for your photo shoot?'

Declan liked the 'we'.

'No,' replied Gnasher. 'But thanks a lot.'

'Yeah, I think we could do some really nice ones on the ornamental bridge. Sort of soft-focus and romantic. And then we could use the footbridge to get some more rock-looking things, and then maybe do some fun shots on the swings and here on the big rocks — you know, two heads peering over boulders and that sort of thing. What do you think?'

'Sounds great to me,' said Gnasher. 'I'll check it with Kelz, but I don't see any problem. And maybe you can come on Friday and take some live action shots?'

'Friday?' asked Laura.

'You mean this big sap didn't tell you we're playing at the Sound Box on Friday?'

'I was going to,' said Declan. 'I just haven't had a chance yet.'

'Anyway, I was hoping you'd both come.'

'I'd love to,' said Laura. 'But I don't want to cramp Mr Donnelly's style.'

'He hasn't got any bloody style.'

'Actually, I was going to ask if you'd come with me,' said Declan.

'I'd love to.'

'Good, then that's settled,' said Gnasher. 'Support local talent.'

'And can I come too, David?' asked Sharon.

'We'll see. Anyway, say good-bye to Declan and Laura. We'd better go home.'

'Bye, Laura,' said Sharon, giving Laura a big hug.

'Bye, Sharon.'

'Bye, Macduff,' said Sharon, throwing her arms around Declan's waist. 'I love you, you know.'

Declan hugged her back. 'Bye, Sharon.'

'You've made a big hit with Sharon,' smiled Laura, as they watched them walk off.

They sat down on the low wall by the entrance to the park.

'How long were you playing badminton?' asked Declan.

'Where did that come from?'

'Just wondering.'

'Ever since primary.'

'And you always went to practice on Wednesday and Friday?'

'Always. Thursdays too, sometimes.'

Declan chuckled and shook his head.

'What's so funny?' asked Laura.

'You know, by that reckoning, I must have passed you a couple of hundred times over the years.'

'So?'

'So how come I never noticed you until I saw you in class?'

'I'm not that noticeable,' replied Laura. 'I mean, I'm not exactly stunning like Sarah or Cass, am I ?' she said honestly. 'I'm just plain old Laura Byrne.'

Declan just looked at her and smiled.

'What?' asked Laura. 'What?'

'You're either fishing for a compliment or —'

'I'm not fishing for anything. I'm being honest.'

'Or, I was going to say,' Declan continued, 'you've been mixing with the wrong people. Those others can't hold a candle to you. Sure, they're attractive, but it's all cultivated from some magazine image. You're naturally attractive. It just shines through from your eyes.'

Laura blushed slightly.

'That's not a come-on line. If we are going to be mates, and I hope we are, I just want to be honest with you. You have what my friend Kumar would call a gentle aura. An aura's —'

'It's OK, Dec. You can't live with my family without knowing about auras, chakras, energies, all that sort of stuff. My mam's big into that, and yoga.'

'Really?'

'But we're not weirdos or anything,' Laura assured him hurriedly.

'It's OK. I wouldn't think you were. I've been practising meditation since the camps, and Mary and the others were really into all that stuff you described. I find it fascinating.'

Laura looked at him and laughed.

'Now it's my turn to ask what's funny,' said Declan.

'Remember when I was raising money to send to Brazil and an anonymous donor gave me thirty-five quid?'

Declan felt himself blushing.

'David wouldn't tell me who it was from. He just said it was from some big fucker who was "nice weird".'

'Charming description.'

'But he did say we should talk because he thought we had a lot in common.'

'He said the same to me.'

'Sounds like he was right, doesn't it?'

Declan nodded.

For a few seconds neither of them said anything. They didn't feel the need to.

'I have a little confession to make, Mr Donnelly,' said Laura softly. 'In the interest of honesty and buddyship.'

'Go on.'

'I was really tempted to come over and talk to you a few

times in school. I don't know why; I just got this feeling that you might be interested in some of the things I was thinking about.'

'And why didn't you?'

'Because sometimes you just seemed cold — like you didn't want anyone near you. As if you thought you were too good for us or something.'

'It wasn't that, honest. It was just that — it's kind of hard, but I promise I'll tell you in time.'

'OK,' she said.

Then they were silent again. Declan looked at the ground, unsure what to do next. Then he remembered something.

'Remember what you were saying on Friday, wondering where you go from here?'

She nodded.

'What about some sort of a fund-raiser to help that place you mentioned?'

'Mukti Ashram?'

'Yes. I remember reading about some kids in America who raised money for a school in India, and there's some Canadian kid who's started some organisation.... Maybe you — we — could do something with them.'

'That's not a bad idea. Maybe we could get Gnasher to do something, a musical or something like that. There's a company in Cork that's doing a play about carpet kids. Maybe we could do something like that. It'd be a start.'

Declan loved the way Laura used the word 'we', but it still scared him a little, getting this close.

'It's an idea. Let's sleep on it,' he said.

Laura took that as a cue to move. She pushed herself up off the wall.

'I suppose we should go. It's starting to get dark and I'm sure you have homework. I know I do.'

They crossed the road to Declan's bus stop.

'See you tomorrow, Declan, and thanks,' smiled Laura.

'Thanks for what?'

'For letting me be your buddy. I was scared of being alone, you know.'

'That makes two of us.'

She smiled and walked off. Declan watched her go. At the corner she turned and waved. He waved back.

As he turned to get on the bus, he saw Conor Meade, Sarah and Cass watching him from across the road. The girls were laughing, but Conor just glared.

Declan paid his fare and started to walk down the bus. He looked towards the building site; Tommy was emerging from behind the bushes.

11

'A girl, then. What do you reckon?'

'Has to be. D'you know, Sean, I even heard him singing in the shower a few minutes ago.'

'Singing? That clinches it. It's a girl.'

Declan looked up from his cereal. His parents had been carrying on the conversation for a few minutes, teasing him. He hadn't risen to the bait so far. That was his part in the game. But he knew the unwritten rules. Now it was his turn.

'Her name's Laura.'

'Laura. Ah,' said his dad, nodding. 'Laura. Be a good name for a granddaughter, that.'

Declan laughed. 'She's just a friend, a buddy. That's it. Plain and simple.'

'That's what all the celebrities say,' announced his mam, taking another sip from her tea. '"We're just good friends." Then they're racing up the aisle like a rabbit chased by a greyhound.'

'She gets that literary turn of phrase from all them Mills and Boons,' said Sean, giving Declan a wink.

'Well, in this case it's true,' said Declan, taking a final spoonful of cereal. He pulled on his blazer on and ran up to the bathroom to brush his teeth, but he could still hear them talking downstairs.

'See, I told you it was nothing to worry about,' his father was saying. 'I said it would just take him time to settle back in after the camps.'

'Maybe you're right,' his mother answered. 'I hope so. I know that's what that Mary one from Nepal said. It just didn't seem natural, him suddenly being all on his own, dropping out of everything, and spending so much time up at that graveyard.'

'Mary said to just give it time. Christy was the same when he came back from Ethiopia, remember? He wasn't his old self for about a year. And Declan didn't even give himself time to mourn for his friend. He just rushed off to them camps.'

'You're probably right. I was just worried that it might be something else.'

'What?'

'I dunno. Just something. But whoever this Laura one is, she's got him back to his old self a bit, *buiochas le Dia.*'

Declan rinsed his mouth and smiled.

He went back downstairs and picked up his bag from the kitchen table.

'Here,' said his father, throwing him the car keys. 'We won't need the old banger today. Maybe you can take Laura for a ride down Lovers' Lane after school.' He made a kissing sound with his lips.

Rose giggled and spluttered tea over her book. 'Now look what the old eejit's made me do.'

'Could I borrow the car Friday night?' Declan asked. 'I'm going to see a couple of kids from school playing with a band in town.'

'Laura going too?' grinned his dad.

Declan just shook his head and laughed.

'Sure, love. We'll be going to bingo in the parish hall.'

'Like hell we will,' replied Sean. 'Chelsea is playing Villa on the box.'

'And you're not coming, then?'

'Not in me Kelly's eye.'

'Well, that's a good one for you. I ...'

Declan left them to it and slipped out of the front door.

❑

As he walked down the corridor, he suddenly began to feel nervous. What if Laura had changed her mind about him? What if she'd got home and decided last night had been a mistake?

He walked into the classroom, picked his usual spot near the back and closed his eyes. Immediately he was back in Nepal.

❑

He was standing beside the jeep, getting ready to leave. Kumar was standing beside him.

'I wish I didn't have to go. I wish I could be here for whatever you do next.'

'I know,' said Kumar. 'But this is our path, Declan. You've got your own path to travel.'

'I just wish I could come with you, just do something.'

'You can do something.' He waved his arm to indicate the camp. 'Look at us. We're just a bunch of nobodies from Bhutan, sitting here rotting, while the rest of the world ignores us. If we had oil or strategic value the West would be in here in a minute. But we have nothing. So does anybody care?'

Declan shook his hand.

'I care.'

'I know you do. That's why you and Mary must go home

and be our voices in Ireland. Let your people know what's happened to us. Ask them to help.'

Declan just nodded.

Kumar lifted a small leather pouch from around his neck.

'In here is soil from Bhutan and from Nepal, mixed together. When you go home, all you have to do is add some Irish soil and we'll be mixed together for ever.'

He motioned to Declan to bend. He lowered his head. Kumar slipped the string holding the pouch over his neck.

'I have to go. I won't say goodbye; that's too final. I'll see you again, I'm sure.'

'Next summer. Maybe in Bhutan.'

'That would be nice,' said Kumar, returning his smile.

Declan watched him walk off, limping: his left hip had been smashed by the rifle-butts of government soldiers, during his imprisonment.

He was about five feet eight, but Declan thought that in many ways he was the biggest man he'd ever met.

❑

'Hi. Daydreaming?'

Declan opened his eyes. Laura was sitting beside him. For a second he was startled.

'You don't mind if I sit here, do you?' she asked uncertainly.

'No. Not at all,' he said apologetically. 'I'd be delighted. I was just miles away there.'

Laura smiled. 'Just say if I start crowding you.'

'That'll never happen. I would —'

They were interrupted by someone banging into the side of the desk, knocking it forward with a shudder. They looked up. Conor was smiling down at Laura.

'Oh, sorry,' he said, ignoring Declan. 'I wasn't watching where I was going.'

Laura just stared at him.

He bent down and put his arm around her. 'A gang of us are going for a coffee after school, Lar. I thought you might fancy coming. We haven't had a chance to talk for a while.'

Laura pushed his arm away roughly. 'No, thanks, I'm busy,' she said curtly. 'Ask Sarah. I'm sure she'd be only too delighted to go with you.'

'Hey, she's no threat to us, babe. She's just a pal.'

Laura laughed dismissively. 'Conor, when will you get it through your head? There isn't an *us* and there never was. We used to play badminton together, that's all.'

'Used to?'

'Yeah, I've quit. '

'When?'

'Right now. And if you don't mind, I was trying to talk to Declan.'

She turned back to Declan. 'As I was saying, maybe at some level — ouch!'

She grimaced. Conor was holding her firmly by the arm. Declan reached out to grab Conor's hand, but as he did he saw a movement out of the corner of his eye. Suddenly Conor went sprawling onto the floor. Gnasher landed on top of him, his school-bag pushed firmly into Conor's face.

'Oh, sorry, mate, I didn't see you there,' said Gnasher, pushing himself up by leaning on his bag.

Conor kicked out at him from the floor, missing. 'You little scumbag, I'll —'

'Gentlemen. When you have quite finished,' called Mr Brady, sweeping into the room, 'I'd like you all to take your seats — and put them on the chairs provided. Then open your books at Chapter Eight, "The Foreign Policy of Bismarck".'

Gnasher sat down behind Declan and Laura. Conor pushed himself up, glaring first at Declan, then at Gnasher. Then he went over to join his friends on the other side of the room.

'You OK?' Declan whispered to Laura.

'Yeah. Conor wouldn't actually mean to hurt me. He didn't even grab me that hard; it was more the surprise. I wish he'd just get it through his head that we were never an item. I don't even really like him that much.'

'Another old habit?'

'Yeah. Listen, I was thinking about something you said last night. Would you like to come down to my house for a coffee at lunchtime? I'd like to talk it over with you.'

'Sure, if that's OK with —'

'Miss Byrne,' said Mr Brady, smiling, 'I'm delighted to see that you have returned to us, and that you are aligning yourself with such exalted company as Mr Donnelly, but if you would be so kind as to leave the dating game until some later time....'

There were hoots of laughter and catcalls from some of the class.

'I really would appreciate the chance to enlighten your tiny minds with the joys of Count Otto Von, as he is known to his friends.'

Laura nodded. 'Sorry, sir.'

Behind her, Gnasher chipped in with 'Lead on, Macduff.'

'Quite, Mr Coyle. Now, the Ems Telegraph....'

For the rest of the double period Declan listened to the intricacies of Otto Von Bismarck's foreign policy. Occasionally he looked across at Laura. He felt happy just being beside her. She caught his glance and smiled.

A couple of times his gaze travelled across the room. Every time it did, Conor seemed to be glaring at him, or whispering to one of his friends and nodding at Declan. Gnasher noticed it too. Towards the end of the period he leaned forward and whispered in Declan's ear, 'You really do seem to be on Meade's mind today, mate. I think you've made an enemy there.'

Declan nodded.

12

Declan watched Laura busily writing down notes. They'd spent lunch brainstorming ideas for ways to help the child bonded labourers. Declan was in awe of Laura's passionate commitment to doing whatever she could to end what she called 'this obscenity'.

They'd come up with a whole list of ideas: a letter-writing campaign to politicians, both in Ireland and in Europe, calling for investigation into the number of products coming into the EU made by child slaves; picketing shops in Dublin that sold carpets made in the sheds; setting up support groups for SACCS in schools across Ireland; organising a fund-raiser for Mukti Ashram. By the time they'd finished, they had a list that ran for two pages.

But they'd prioritised two ideas. The first was to start an education group in school, like the Amnesty Group, devoted to the issue of bonded labour. The second was to get involved in a new campaign Laura had found on the Global March website, which called on governments to support the call for free education for every child in the Third World. Laura wanted to get every kid in Ireland to sign a petition to be sent to the Minister of Foreign Affairs, calling on him to put pressure on governments to introduce compulsory free education in all countries where bonded labour existed.

'We could do that as a start, and maybe get someone like Bono or Bob Geldof interested in the petition as well,' she said enthusiastically.

She was so excited that she'd hardly touched her sandwich, and she couldn't have had more than two sips of her coffee.

Declan looked at his watch. 'You have me so exhausted by all this work, Miss Byrne, that I think we should head back to school for a rest.'

Laura took another sip from her now-cold coffee. 'Right, Mr Donnelly, after you.'

As they walked up the drive towards the green, someone behind them called, 'Laura!'

They looked back. Conor was hurrying towards them. He was on his own.

'Hi, Conor,' said Laura.

'Laura, can I talk to you?'

'Sure. It's OK if he walks up with us, isn't it, Declan?'

Declan nodded.

'No. It's important. I really need to talk to you alone,' Conor said, looking at Declan.

'It's OK,' said Declan. 'I'll just walk on a bit. You can catch me up.'

'Fine. I will,' said Laura. 'In a few seconds.'

As he walked on, Declan heard the beginning of what Conor was saying. 'I was talking to Jason last night....'

He didn't hear the rest. He felt the pain between his legs; his stomach began to cramp and that old breathlessness came back. He tried to walk on. He'd been wrong. It had all been a mistake. She would hear all about him and dump him. He should have stayed on his own.

He heard Laura shouting angrily and looked back.

'Just get away from me and stay away, you little creep!'

she called, storming off. Conor tried to grab her arm, but she shrugged out of the way.

'Laura, it's true, I swear,' he shouted after her.

'Come near us again and, so help me, I'll brain you. Now get lost.'

Conor was falling back to join Sarah and Cass. Laura hurried up to join Declan. She was flushed with anger.

'What was that all about?' asked Declan.

'Nothing. Just Conor being his normal creepy self,' she replied, loud enough for anyone around to hear.

'Was he talking about me?'

'It was more a case of what he was saying about himself, if you ask me.'

'But what did he say?'

She reached out and took Declan's hand. 'Nothing worth listening to.'

'Maybe we should talk about it,' he offered nervously.

'We'll decide what we talk about and when, not little creeps like him. Agreed?'

Declan sighed, relieved. 'Agreed!'

❑

Declan found out exactly what Conor had been telling Laura at the end of school. Second period after lunch, Conor had excused himself from class to go to the loo. Declan hadn't thought anything of it at the time; but when he went to his locker at the end of school, he saw Gnasher trying to scrub something off it with a wet rag. He was doing quite a good job, but Declan could still make out the words scribbled in felt marker. 'QUEER' was written in the largest letters. Of course, he couldn't prove Conor had done that, but the rest of the message gave a hint: 'KEEP AWAY FROM LAURA.'

'Sorry you had to see this, mate,' said Gnasher.

Declan was sorry too.

'I reckon you know who did it, don't you?' Gnasher asked.

Declan turned around. Conor and some of his crowd were leaning against a wall, watching and sniggering.

'Yeah,' he said, looking straight at them and speaking in cool, measured tones. 'Some little weasel with as much guts as his loudmouth brother, but even less brainpower, if that's possible.'

Conor reddened. Then he turned and walked off with his pals, sniggering.

'You should have decked him,' said Gnasher. 'Or let me do it for you.'

'That wouldn't have got rid of this,' said Declan, pointing to the graffiti. 'And anyway, he's not worth the effort.'

'You are some cool cookie,' said Gnasher.

Declan nodded, picked up the wet rag and started scrubbing at the graffiti. He felt anything but cool.

'Hi. Whatcha doing?'

Declan turned around. Tommy was looking at them. His school-bag was dangling on the floor, as usual, and he was eating a Snickers bar.

'We're finger-painting,' said Gnasher. 'What does it look like we're doing? Prat.'

'Cleaning.' Tommy looked at the graffiti. 'Who's the queer?'

'Just give us a hand or piss off,' replied Gnasher.

'I only came to see Declan.'

'Let me guess. You want me to give you some extra coaching.'

'Yeah. You're the best in the club.'

'Don't tell Jason. He thinks that's him.'

'He's just a sap.'

'Let me think about it.'

'Right,' grinned Tommy. 'I'm off to detention. See you again.'

He swung his bag over his shoulder and walked off, whistling.

'He doesn't seem too worried about detention,' said Declan, watching him go.

'Why should he?' replied Gnasher. 'He spends as much time there as he does at home.'

Declan turned back to the graffiti. 'You know ...' he started. His words were cut off by the sound of someone banging the back of the locker. He and Gnasher jumped.

'Good to see you're getting into practice for your career, Declan,' sneered Jason Meade as he walked into the changing-room. 'The world needs good cleaners. Keep up the good work.'

'What a plonker,' said Gnasher. 'Come on, let's get a quick coffee.'

❏

Tommy was the last kid in the corridor. He'd been held back at the end of detention for one of Mr McCormack's little lectures about eating crisps in class, and now he'd earned himself another detention as well. It wasn't fair! He hadn't been cheeky or impolite. He'd just wanted to know, again, why he shouldn't be allowed to eat in class if it didn't disrupt his schoolwork and didn't disturb anyone else — and it hadn't done either — and then suggested that 'Because that's the school rule' wasn't really a very satisfactory answer.

What was the point of the principal telling you that now you were in secondary you'd be treated like an adult, if the response to a reasonable question was to punish you as if you were a cheeky kid? Tommy didn't get that at all.

As he went down the corridor, he looked through the window and saw Declan heading across the playground to collect his car. He quickened his pace. He didn't run — there were two teachers and a prefect in the corridor, and he didn't want another detention — but he *hurried* out the door. Declan was by his car. Tommy started to run towards him.

'What the fu —'

A hand grabbed him by the hair and dragged him around the corner, pushing him roughly up against the wall.

'We got any more goodies in the bag like that drink the other morning?' demanded Jason Meade. He pushed his face so close to Tommy's that their noses were almost touching.

Oh, no, Tommy moaned to himself. *Now I'll get it.*

Meade grabbed the bag out of his hand and opened it. He pulled out a can of Coke.

'This'll do. I'd have preferred another nice cold Lucozade, but ...'

Tommy didn't hear what he said next. He almost sagged with relief. *The prat hasn't a clue! Thank God!*

'What you laughing at, you little poof?' snapped Meade.

He put his foot on Tommy's toe. Tommy wriggled his foot out of his shoe. Meade bent down and picked it up.

'Let's give Declan a pressie.'

He took aim and slung the shoe at Declan's car. Then he lifted Tommy's bag over his head and started swinging it around.

'Jason, don't, please don't,' Tommy begged. He didn't actually mean it. He didn't see what throwing his shoe or his bag across the car park was actually supposed to do to him, but it was obviously part of Meade's idea that he should grovel and plead, so he did.

'Please don't, Jason.' *Sap!*

❑

Declan climbed into his car and turned on the radio.

'And I told you once
And I told you twice
And I'm telling you once again....'

The sound of the Legendary Stone Mountain Band jumped from the speakers. Declan knew the band and the song, but not by choice: his father kept the radio tuned to one of those illegal country-music stations that seem to have three albums which they play over and over again, and any time he turned it on they seemed to be playing something from the *I Really Hate Merle Haggard* album by the Legendary Stone Mountain Band. He'd heard worse. He leaned forward and changed stations to Lite FM.

'The drugs don't —'

Richard Ashcroft's voice was interrupted by something banging down on the bonnet of the car. It was a kid's shoe. Declan looked in his rear-view mirror. Tommy was racing across the car park, wearing only one shoe. Jason Meade was behind him. He had Tommy's school-bag over his head, spinning it around like a hammer-thrower.

Bastard.

Meade took careful aim and then let go. The bag landed somewhere behind Declan's car. Tommy started towards it.

For a second Declan was tempted to get out and try to stop it, but he didn't. That would make it worse. If Meade thought he liked Tommy, he'd probably bully him even more, just as another way of humiliating Declan.

He had to convince Meade that he didn't care what he did to Tommy. Maybe then he'd leave the poor kid alone.

He started the engine and checked his rear-view mirror again. Tommy was still some way off.

'Sorry, Tommy. Nothing too breakable, I hope.' He reversed slowly, feeling the bump as he drove over the bag. The bag burst and the contents scattered all over the playground.

Tommy couldn't believe it. He was sure Declan had seen what had happened, but he knew he must have been wrong. Declan wouldn't have done that on purpose.

Declan didn't stop. He drove straight out of the gates. In

his side-mirror he could see Tommy scrambling around to pick up the books and things that had been scattered.

'That's a real hero, huh?' laughed Meade, as Declan drove off.

Sap, Tommy thought. *He's worth a thousand of you any day.*

13

'Wednesday, weird Wednesday,' Declan sang to himself as he drove the car up the road towards the school. It had been weird. Over the last few days, school had come to mean seeing Laura at break, talking to Gnasher in class and between classes, and trying to avoid Tommy. A sort of normality had grown up around that routine. But this morning none of that had been there. Laura hadn't come into school; she was at the hospital for a check-up. Gnasher and Kelz had taken time off to do some practice for the gig at the Sound Box; and Declan had seen Tommy heading up the road in the morning, but he hadn't seen him since. Of course, there were other people to nod to and have brief exchanges, and Conor Meade was right there to glare at him and whisper about him, but Declan missed the familiarity of the others. A hole had been punched in his day. He'd even startled his parents by going home for lunch.

As he turned the corner into the rear car park, he kept an eye out for Tommy.

I wouldn't put it past that mad little prat to suddenly jump out at me, he thought with a grin, as he pulled into a parking-space.

❏

Tommy lifted the coat off the hook in the changing-room, rolled it up and pushed it into his bag. He hated doing it — he didn't want to be a thief — but he didn't have a choice. He needed it. Anyway, he wasn't really stealing it. He was just borrowing it for a few hours, until he could get home and get the duvet off his bed.

His heart was beating hard as he sneaked out of the changing-room and slipped along the corridor. Just as he reached the door, it swung open. Tommy's heart leapt with fear. Then he saw who'd opened the door: it was Meade. He was carrying a basketball.

'Hey, I want a word with you, scumbag,' said Meade

'Sure, Jase,' said Tommy, going out. 'But can it wait till later?'

'No, it bloody can't,' snapped Meade. He grabbed Tommy by the tie and hauled him around the corner of the building.

Now what? Tommy wondered. *Maybe someone squealed about the Lucozade.... Nah, no one would do that. Just play along with the sap.*

Meade grabbed him by the throat, almost lifting him off his feet.

'What's this about you going behind everyone's back and trying to get that big poof, Donnelly, to coach the second-years?' he spat. 'He's not even part of the club any more. The traitor walked out on us.'

'We were just thinking ...' wheezed Tommy.

Meade loosened his grip, picked up the basketball and started bouncing it off Tommy's head, hard. Tommy's throat was sore. He could still feel the pressure of Meade's thumb against his Adam's apple. For the first time, he was really scared of him.

'You don't *think*, scumbag. It's not your job to think.'

Declan parked in his usual place, locked the doors and started walking towards the students' entrance.

'I wasn't doing anything, honestly, Jase.'

He heard Tommy's voice coming from behind the edge of the block. Then he heard a soft *thud, thud, thud*, like the sound óf someone heading a football.

'You were betraying the club, you little queer.'

Declan walked around the corner and stopped. Meade wasn't just bouncing the ball off Tommy's head. He was slamming it. The urge to grab Meade and do the same to him was almost overwhelming, but Declan had to resist.

'What's this?' laughed Meade, staring at Declan. 'Hero to the rescue? You weren't much of a hero last time, were you, Deckie?' He moved his hips suggestively.

Tommy looked at Declan, pleading with his eyes.

'Meade,' Declan said, trying to sound casual, 'if this is how you get your kicks these days, have fun.'

'Too right I will,' said Meade. He grabbed the end of Declan's tie and flicked it up into his face. Declan shrugged and walked away.

He went quickly into the corridor. A bunch of fourth-year rugby players were outside the changing-room, waiting for it to be opened.

Declan put his hand in his pocket and whipped out a five-pound note. 'This is for the first guy to run around the school anticlockwise, from the small car park behind us to back here.'

'No joke?'

'No joke. I swear,' said Declan.

The door opened and they rushed out, yelling.

Declan smiled at the thought of Meade looking up to see that lot bearing down on him. He felt sick to his stomach that he had had to leave Tommy like that; but maybe now the kid would leave him alone, and then Meade would leave Tommy alone.

As he made his way towards the art room, Declan looked back. Tommy was coming down the corridor, rubbing his throat. For once he wasn't smiling to himself. He looked quite shaken.

He saw Declan and called out to him, 'Have you thought about it yet?' But it seemed to be almost a reflex, lacking in any real enthusiasm.

Declan sat down on a step. *What would it take?*

'Tommy, why do you want me to teach you? Why not Tracey or Keating or any of the sixth-years?'

'Because you're the best player this school's ever seen.'

Declan laughed.

'Who said that, my mam?'

'No, Doc did. He told us one night when you were off sick. He said if we wanted to be really great players we should try to be like you, 'cause you were the best there ever was in this school.'

At the thought of Doc standing in front of a bunch of first-years and singing his praises, Declan felt his eyes begin to moisten.

'And if I wasn't the best? Would you still want me to teach you?'

'But you are,' Tommy said flatly.

'If I wasn't, would you stop asking?'

'Sure,' shrugged Tommy. 'But you are.'

'Right. Stay and watch the senior practice tonight. Deal?' He held out his hand.

'Deal,' said Tommy, without smiling.

Declan got up to go, then stopped. 'Is there something else on your mind?'

Tommy looked at Declan and part of him felt like crying. This was the guy he'd idolised, the guy he'd thought was the hottest thing since sliced bread. Could he really have been that wrong? A few minutes ago, Declan had just stood there as Meade bounced that basketball off Tommy's head. And

then he'd let himself be humiliated, treated like a complete
wimp. This was all wrong.

'Why did you let Meade do that — treat you like that,
Declan? He's such a creep. Why?'

'You wouldn't understand, Tommy. You really
wouldn't.'

'Try me.'

Declan started to walk away. He could see the hurt, the
disappointment in Tommy's eyes, but there was nothing he
could do about that. It would be easier for Tommy, in the
long run.

'I'll see you tonight.'

'OK. I'll tell the others.' Tommy started to head off in the
other direction.

'And, Tommy,' Declan called after him.

Tommy turned around.

'Make sure you keep away from Meade and his pals.'

'Those arseholes,' said Tommy. 'Seems like you should
keep away from them, too.'

14

Once, there'd been two Declan Donnellys. One could sprint the length of the basketball court, the ball seeming almost an extension of his arm, as he wove and spun past the opposition before leaping up to score. The other did everything else. It was as if, when he peeled off his street clothes to get ready for a game, the everyday Declan came away with them and was left behind in a locker until the game was over.

Out on the court only one thing mattered: the game. Nothing else intruded — no worries, no uncertainties, no noise in the hall. Out there, the only thing he was aware of was the movement of the other nine players on the court.

At least, that was how it used to be. But not tonight.

Declan didn't want to be there. He'd had to force himself. It had been one thing walking past the changing-room on his way down the corridor, or storming into it in anger as he had the other day; but to actually go inside with the purpose of getting changed to play basketball.... His hand shook as he reached for the door. Just being there brought it all back — the sounds, the pain, the terror, the dull aching sickness. He wanted to turn and run.

He forced himself to get changed and step out onto the court with the others, but he was only half there. It was as if his eyes weren't focusing properly: one was watching the game, the other was seeing all the ghosts in this place. All night he'd been bumping into memories — Doc passing to him, Doc turning players for him, Doc and him playing one-on-one, Doc everywhere he turned. And every other memory kept bringing him back to That Night.

This must be what insanity is like.

The gym door slammed shut. Declan froze. The ball bounced away from him. Before he could react, Bobby Curry had snatched it and started a movement up the court. It had been like that all night. People he used to coach were running rings around him.

'Oh, brilliant, Donnelly,' sniggered a voice from the doorway.

Declan felt a knot in the pit of his stomach.

He didn't have to turn around. He knew where they'd be, Meade, Brendan O'Connor, Phil Cahill and a couple of the other so-called veterans: they'd be leaning against the door in a tight knot, laughing and sniggering to each other, moving their half-closed fists up and down in an obscene gesture. He'd seen them do it a thousand times before.

He could feel himself beginning to shake.

What did he expect? He'd come back to this place, the place where it had all happened, a place where he knew they'd be. He hadn't expected it to be plain sailing.

But he hadn't known it would be like this, either.

'Remember, Declan, fear is only a reaction.' It was Kumar's voice, coming from somewhere in his memory, bringing him back to a night when they'd sat in Kumar's hut and Declan had asked about his time in a Bhutanese jail.

'But weren't you frightened?' he'd asked.

'Of course I was,' Kumar had said. 'I'm not Superman. But I'd read a book by a man called Primo Levi, who'd been

in a concentration camp in World War II. They'd stripped
him of everything; but then one day he realised he still had
one thing left. They hadn't taken his right to choose how he
reacted to the fact that they'd taken everything from him.'

'I don't get that.'

'Neither did I, at first. It took me months. Then I realised
that, no matter what anyone did to me, they couldn't make
me afraid unless I allowed them to. I could choose to feel or
not to feel fear.'

'I still don't get it,' Declan had said.

Kumar had smiled. 'Don't try to get it. Just keep remind-
ing yourself that fear is just an emotion, and you don't have
to let anyone else control your emotions.'

Declan had sort of got it.

He knew he hadn't been in control of his own emotions
That Night, with Doc; or that first time, three years ago.
They had. Both times they'd taken complete control. He'd
begged, and cried like a baby, but it had made no difference.
They'd carried on, enjoying his fear, owning him.

Instinctively, he fingered the pouch around his neck as he
forced himself to turn around. There they were, just as he'd
imagined them, standing at the door of the gym, smirking.

The whistle blew.

'OK, lads, stay here, all apart from Declan. Declan, you
can hit the showers.'

Declan glanced at the benches at the far end of the hall.
When the game had started, the second-year and third-year
teams had all been there, waiting eagerly to see his return.
Now Tommy was the only one left. Declan hadn't noticed
them going, but he couldn't blame them. Maybe now
Tommy would stop hassling him.

He headed for the changing-room, keeping his eyes
firmly focused on the door, trying to stare through Meade
and the others. The small, tight fist of fear in his stomach
was growing bigger with every step.

'Declan.'

He stopped. Bob Fitzsimons was coming towards him.

'Sorry to send you off, son, but it just wasn't happening for you tonight, was it?'

'I told you, sir.'

'I thought that was just an excuse to miss training.'

'I've never done that, sir, honest.'

'No, I know,' Bob said. 'But put yourself in my position: You've got an inter-county player with a scholarship to a major American university, and he's telling you he can't play any more. Would you believe him? Of course not. You'd think he was just being lazy or something. But tonight ...'

He let the words trail off, using the silence to emphasise his disappointment.

'Even professional athletes can suddenly have a dip in form, and you have been out of school for a year; but you were ...' He lowered his voice and smiled wryly. 'You were pretty bad out there.'

Declan couldn't help smiling. 'I stank, sir. Thanks for the honesty.'

'What's happened? Was it Doc?'

Declan would have liked to be honest with him, but there was no way to do that. 'I suppose so, sir. It's all just sort of gone, since Doc.'

'Yeah, I felt that way too for quite a while.'

For a moment there was nothing else they could say. They were both thinking about a big, lanky kid with dark hair and a goatee.

'But you know, maybe if you keep coming it'll all start to come back. I'm sure Doc wouldn't have wanted you to let it slip. Maybe all it'll take is a bit of concentration on your own. Maybe in a few weeks?'

'Sure, maybe.'

They could have traded maybes all night. They both knew the truth: Declan would never play again.

'There's nothing else, is there, Dec? You know, nothing outside? Everything's all right at home — your mam, your dad, they're OK?'

'Home's fine, sir.'

'And school? That's going OK?'

'As well as it is for anyone else.'

'If there is anything — you know, any problem ...'

Declan shook his head.

'OK. Hit the showers. I presume I can tell Doug Regan you won't be attending the final Dublin trials tomorrow.'

'Sorry.'

'So am I, Declan, believe me. So am I.'

He headed for the changing-room door again. He felt as if he was about to vomit.

'Off for an early set and blow-dry, sweetie?' sniggered Meade. The others grinned as they blocked Declan's way.

Declan felt his stomach cramp getting worse.

'You know something, Meade?' He forced himself to laugh. 'You should donate your brain to medical research. They'd pay top price for it.'

'Why, 'cause I'm so brilliant?'

'No, 'cause it's never been used.'

The others laughed, but Jason Meade flushed angrily. He stepped forward to face Declan, only a foot or two away. O'Connor, Cahill and Don Rafferty gathered around in a semicircle. Declan planted his feet firmly on the ground, like a defender protecting the net against an oncoming forward. His heart was racing; his hands were moist and clammy. His throat was suddenly dry.

He couldn't back down for them, no matter how scared he was. They were the same as any pack: let them smell fear and they'd come in for the kill. Tonight, he'd be in control of his own emotions, if only for a few seconds.

He stared into Jason Meade's eyes, not blinking, not flinching. For a second, Declan thought he saw something in

Meade's look, something he'd seen in the shopping mall, but he still couldn't name it. Then it was gone.

'Mr Meade, if you want to play, get out here now,' called Bob Fitzsimons.

Meade moved, as if to let Declan pass, but at the last moment he shifted his weight onto one foot and bumped into him, shoulder to chest. He put his hand out as if to steady Declan, but instead his hand went between his legs. He grabbed Declan's testicles and squeezed hard. 'Later, sweetie!' he laughed.

Declan spun around angrily, ready to lash out, but Meade had already sprinted into the middle of the gym. Declan glared at him, but he just blew a kiss and laughed. So did his friends. Some of the other sixth-years were laughing too.

Declan flushed with anger. He glanced at the bench. Tommy was looking at the ground.

Declan slammed angrily into the changing-room. His hands shook with temper as he pulled off his vest and threw himself heavily onto the bench. Meade and the others had dumped their gear all over the bench, so that everyone could see the brand names on their towels and deodorants, and their screw-top isotonic drink bottles. The urge to grab them and smash them into a thousand pieces was almost irresistible.

He slammed his hands palms-down against the bench.

'Damn!'

He heard the door open slowly, but he didn't look up. He was furious with himself. He'd let Meade do it again. 'Damn!'

'Declan?' Tommy said cautiously. 'Are you OK?'

Declan glared at him.

'Great! Huh, Tommy? Wasn't I? The best player who ever played for the school. Fantastic! Absolutely fantastic!'

He was almost spitting the words, but Tommy didn't notice the irony.

'You just had a bit of bad luck, that's all. You were a bit tired or something. But if you practise with us for a while —'

'For God's sake, Tommy,' exploded Declan, jumping to his feet, 'how stupid are you? What will it take to make you see how crap I am? Wake up! I'm useless, and even if I wasn't, I wouldn't want to teach a bunch of whiners like you and your mates.'

Tommy started to say something, but Declan kept screaming.

'Get it through your thick little skull! I don't want anything to do with any of you!'

Tommy began to back off. There were tears in his eyes. Declan followed him.

'So go on, Tommy. Piss off. Go home. Stop being so irritating. Just go!'

Tommy ran, crying. He stopped at the door.

'Do you want to know what I think, Declan?' he shouted.

'No, but that's not going to stop you telling me,' Declan shouted back.

'The wrong one died in that crash. It should have been you. I wish it had been.'

He walked out and slammed the door.

Declan flopped down onto his bench.

'I wish it too, Tommy. I really do.'

He pulled off the rest of his things, found his shower gel, shampoo and towel and went to the showers.

He was feeling cheap and empty. He liked Tommy. He really did. And he'd just dumped all over him, reducing the kid to tears. He could justify it all he liked, telling himself he was trying to protect him, but he hadn't needed to be that rough. He knew that.

The water was cool. He shivered as it hit the back of his neck and ran down his spine. He poured shampoo into his hand and rubbed it onto his hair. One of the changing-room doors opened quietly, and a big dark shadow crossed towards

the bench; then another door banged open, and immediately
Jason Meade was shouting tauntingly.

'Hey, Donnelly! I think it's about time you and I got
down to our unfinished business.'

Declan saw Meade's yellow vest rushing towards him.
Then the shampoo trickled into his eyes. He closed his eyes,
blinded. Instinctively he clenched his fists and raised his
arms to cover his head. There was a sound of running feet,
and then suddenly Meade's shout was cut off in a strangled
gasp.

Declan wiped the shampoo from his eyes and blinked
them open. Jason Meade was pinned to the wall by a huge
hand that held him around the throat. His feet were dangling
off the ground and his eyes were wide in fear; his hands
clung desperately to the hand holding him.

'I thought I was meeting you outside,' said Declan,
smiling.

'I got bored waiting and came to find you,' replied the
giant figure in black.

The giant loosened his grip, and Jason Meade fell to the
ground.

'Who the fuck are you?' he gasped, pushing himself into
a sitting position and rubbing his throat with his hand.

'Donnelly,' said the giant, standing over him smiling.
'Christy Donnelly. Nice to meet you. Now, what's this
unfinished business we have?'

Declan smiled. 'I don't think you've met my nephew
Christy before, have you?' he said sweetly. 'No, hang on —
you have. About three years ago. The night I played my first
game for the seniors. Remember? I was just a big, skinny
kid, and you were — what? sixteen? seventeen?'

Meade tried to push himself up, but Christy placed a size
fifteen foot on his shoulder and he slunk back down onto the
floor.

'You mean this little weasel was one of the guys who

jumped you in the shower, grabbed your balls and pissed on you?' asked Christy.

Declan nodded, letting the water wash the shampoo from his body. He had eventually told Christy about that first night, but only the edited version, and he'd sworn never to tell anyone else.

'I told you then, you should let me break their bleeding necks. Want me to do it now?' he asked, rubbing the toe of his boot menacingly along the side of Jason Meade's face.

Declan looked at Meade. He was actually crying.

Is this what we were scared of?

'I don't think so. He's not worth the effort, Chris.'

'It wouldn't be an effort, Dec, honest. I wouldn't even break a sweat.'

Suddenly, the bravado was gone. This didn't mean anything, Meade whinging on the floor. It wasn't a victory — not for Declan. Sometime, tomorrow, the next day, he'd meet Meade without Christy.

The pain in his stomach almost bent him double. He fought hard not to let it show.

'I'd better get changed. We've got places to go,' he said, fighting to control the quiver in his voice. *Not now. Not here. You can't lose it now.*

As he stepped out of the shower and reached for his towel, his hand trembled.

'Now be a good boy and shout sorry to my Uncle Declan, before you crawl back to your hole,' said Christy.

'Sorry, Declan,' sniffed Meade.

'Now go. Your sins are forgiven,' said Christy, and he made the sign of the cross over Meade.

As Meade scrambled out of the door, Christy sat down on the bench opposite Declan.

'You OK?'

'Yeah,' Declan lied. His heart was beating like a drum machine. They could still reduce him to tears.

'You don't look it.'

'I'm fine, honest.'

'Well, if you need to talk, you know it goes with my job.' Christy pulled off his scarf with a flourish, to show his clerical collar.

He took a cigar and a box of matches from the pocket of his black overcoat. He put the cigar in his mouth, lit the match by flicking it on his thumbnail, held it against the cigar and inhaled deeply.

'The last one from Granda's gift box,' he smiled. 'Strangest ordination present I got.'

'My father's one of a kind,' Declan said, forcing a smile.

'You know, I enjoyed playing hard man with that little creep. He had "bully" written all over his swagger.'

'I thought you were supposed to love everyone, Father Donnelly.'

'Oh, I do,' smiled Christy, blowing rings of smoke up towards the ceiling. 'Some people are bloody impossible to like, but I love them all the same.'

'You should have skipped the Church and become a hit man for the Mob.'

'I thought about it,' said Christy. 'But the guy upstairs has more clout. Maybe I'll get a job in Rome. Papal enforcer, that'd do me grand. Now will you get dressed and let's go for this pint. I've been dying of thirst ever since I got back from Ethiopia.'

'That was more than a year ago!'

'Yeah, but it was awful hot out there.'

15

It was quarter past three in the morning, and Declan was still awake. His whole body was soaked in sweat and his heart was pounding. He lay there, fingering the pouch around his neck, looking at the ceiling.

Oh God, Kumar! Why didn't you say, 'Yes, Declan, you should stay'? Why didn't you talk me out of coming home? It was safe with you. I didn't have to face this crap.

It hadn't even been a dream this time. He'd been wide awake. He'd seen the whole thing in living colour. He could feel the pain in his buttocks and that awful sickening cramp in his stomach.

❑

The boy is thirteen, and tall for his age. His thin frame and narrow shoulders make him look awkward and gangly, but he moves with the grace of a ballet dancer — controlling the ball with his right hand, confidently switching it to his left as he spins around his opponent and begins his movement down the court. He seems totally unconcerned that he is a third-year playing in the sixth-year team. He is as good as any, better than most. 'A natural if ever I saw one,' the coach whispers to someone beside him. Time and time again the boy turns, sprints, shimmies his way past players, putting himself in shooting positions. When he shoots, he shoots single-handed, double-handed, distance shots and slams. He is never off target.

The whistle for the end of the game sounds. The boy turns and waves to his father, his brother and his nephew Christy, before heading off to the changing-room with the rest of the team.

He sits down next to a tall, thin boy with a goatee: the team captain, Kieran 'Doc' Docherty.

'Welcome to the big boys,' grins Doc, hugging him with one arm.

The boy smiles. 'Thanks.'

'Good game, Declan,' says the coach. 'Welcome to the senior team.' Most of the team cheer and hoot and clap, with Doc acting as cheerleader.

The boy blushes and says 'Thanks' again.

The coach turns and looks at some of the older players.

'Mr Meade, Mr O'Connor and Mr Cahill — you could all learn a lot from Declan's unselfish play. That's how I want to see you playing from now on. This is a team game, gentlemen, I believe I have mentioned that before. If you want to be solo stars, try badminton or boxing. But in a team game we pass to the others. What do we do, Mr Meade?'

'Pass,' mumbles Jason Meade.

'Mr O'Connor?'

'Pass.'

'Mr Cahill?'

'I was passing, sir,' Cahill protests.

The teacher looks at him. 'Yes, I know you were, Mr Cahill, but only to Messrs Meade and O'Connor. It's a five-man game. You also have to pass to the other two. We were lucky there tonight: Doc and young Declan worked well together, otherwise we could have been stuffed. Declan's a natural target man. Use him in future ... or buy a pair of boxing gloves.'

The coach turns away. The boy looks up. Jason Meade is glaring at him. The boy turns away quickly. He is nervous.

'OK, hit the showers. Doc, can I see you a second?'

The boy strips off and gets into the shower. Soapy water rolls down his naked body. He feels happier than he's ever felt. He's made the senior team and he has played well. It is a wonderful feeling.

Suddenly hands grab him, pushing his arms high up behind his back, forcing his face down towards the floor. He tries to shout, but a wet towel is jammed against his mouth, cutting off his words.

A voice whispers in his ear: 'Welcome to the big boys, Declan.'

Something long and hard is rammed roughly between his buttocks and into his back passage. He feels as if his whole lower body is being ripped apart. The pain sears through his body, setting his brain on fire. It is worse than a thousand tooth-nerves being touched at once.

He screams, but the towel cuts off his words.

Jason Meade twists the tube. Then he slips his hands between the boy's legs, fondling. Involuntarily, the boy stiffens.

Oh Jesus!

'The little queer's enjoying it,' laughs Meade. 'He's loving it.'

'Yeah, welcome to the big boys,' says Cahill.

Tears flood the boy's eyes. He screams, howling into the towel, begging them to stop.

'For Christ's sake!' a voice shouts from across the changing-room. It's Doc.

As suddenly as it started, the assault ends. The towel is pulled away from the boy's mouth and the hard deodorant can is yanked free from his buttocks. It falls to the bottom of the shower. The boy collapses against the wall, sobbing, and slithers to the floor.

'You bunch of bloody arseholes,' roars Doc, pushing Meade and the others out of the way.

'We were just having a laugh.' Meade sniggers.

'Just welcoming to the club. Jumping him in, like we was all jumped in,' says Cahill.

'We said that crap was finished,' shouts Doc. 'Over!'

'Oops. Must have forgotten,' giggles Meade.

'Get out! Get out and get changed, now,' Doc orders.

He sits down beside the boy, putting his arm around him. 'You OK, Dec? They didn't really mean anything,' says Doc soothingly. 'They were honestly just messing. Welcoming you to the club.'

'It's OK, really,' sniffs the boy, lying. The pain makes him want to vomit. But if this is what everyone went through, he will not be any different. Doc gently rubs his shoulder as if he were a baby.

Suddenly, the boy is embarrassed. Something else is happening, involuntarily. He puts his hands down to cover between his legs, hoping no one will notice. He is so ashamed.

'Is it really OK?' asks Doc.

'Yeah, honest,' he sniffs, through the pain and the confusion and the embarrassment.

'You're a good kid.' Doc stands up and helps him to his feet. 'But don't say anything about this, Dec. It's sort of the team code that messing like that doesn't get mentioned outside the changing-room.'

The boy nods. How could he tell anyone? He prays no one else will say anything.

'That won't happen again, I promise,' says Doc.

He leads the boy to the bench and helps him sit down. Sitting is painful. The boy winces.

'I'm warning you bastards,' says Doc, looking at everyone in turn. 'This crap is finished. Now and forever, right?'

The others nod. Some of the other guys gather around Declan, rubbing his head, patting him on the shoulder, making sympathetic noises. Meade and his friends stay in their own corner, laughing.

❑

'Where'd you get that crap, Doc?' Declan whispered into the darkness. 'We should have told. That wasn't messing. That was sexual abuse — serious sexual abuse. Balls to your code! Look where it got us. And those bastards are just carrying on the same way. Thanks a lot, pal.'

Declan went down to the kitchen. He made himself a cup of coffee and sat down at the breakfast bar, staring at the wall.

Doc had looked after him, just as he'd promised. In those first few days after they'd come for him, Declan had been so full of fear and shame that he hadn't wanted to be in school. Left to himself, he'd have just stayed in a corner and whimpered, like a frightened puppy; but Doc hadn't let him. He'd sought him out at break and at lunch and made sure he was never alone, spent ages just being with him, hanging around talking about nothing in particular. And Declan had followed him around like a puppy, waiting for him outside his classes, changing routes between classes just so he could see him.

And Meade and his mates hadn't come near him again. Sometimes they'd given him dirty looks, and maybe if he was passing one of them would 'accidentally' bump into him or one of their bags would fall in front of him and trip him; but there had never been anything like that first time again. Not until That Night.

And that hadn't been Doc's fault.

Yes, it fucking was!

Suddenly, Declan couldn't help it. He was furious — furious with Doc.

It was his fault; everything that had happened to him over the last three years was Doc's fault.

It was Doc who'd had him jumped up two teams. If that hadn't happened, life would have gone on as normal. He'd have gone through the school system being just another basketball player. Meade and his friends wouldn't have been humiliated in the changing-room because of him, and they wouldn't have started to hate him. If Doc hadn't brought the UHT professor to see them play basketball, there would never have been a scholarship and Declan would never have beaten Meade to it. If Doc had told after the first time they came at Declan, instead of hushing it up because of that 'code', something could have been done about Meade and the others. They'd have been punished for what they'd done, maybe expelled or even taken to court. And That Night wouldn't have happened.

And after That Night Doc went and died. How the hell could he drive a car into a tree he'd passed a hundred times already? By accident? Maybe. But what if it was on purpose, what if he was running away from what had happened? How could he leave me to face it all on my own? How could he just take the easy way out?

Declan was shaking with anger. It was all Doc's fault. It was. It was.

He couldn't take this; he had to talk to someone. He looked at the clock. 4.00am. It would be 9.00am in Nepal.

He went into the hall, picked up the phone and dialled. After a few seconds, a male voice answered.

'Kumar?'

'Yes?'

'It's Declan.'

'Declan! How are you?'

'I —' He stumbled, and then he began to cry.

By the time he hung up, he'd been on the phone to Kumar for more than an hour — sometimes weeping, sometimes laughing as they remembered things that had happened in the camp, sometimes talking. Kumar had hardly spoken. He'd made the odd comment that would help Declan to continue, but most of the time he'd just listened, as Declan told him everything about the first night, about That Night, about his fear and confusion over Laura, Tommy, Gnasher. Everything just came tumbling out.

But at the end of the conversation Declan felt relieved, as if he'd been holding his breath for a very long time and he'd finally taken a huge lungful of fresh air.

'I'm glad you finally decided to tell me, Declan.'

'So am I.'

'May I make one suggestion?' Kumar said. 'Find someone over there to share your secret with. A burden shared is a burden halved.'

Declan laughed. 'Is this the Zen master again?'

'No,' replied Kumar. 'I found that in a Christmas cracker when I was in California. But it sounds good if you say it with enough seriousness, doesn't it?'

'Who should I tell?'

'Follow your heart.'

'Another Christmas cracker?'

'No, a song by some old country band — the Legendary Stone Mountain Band. But it makes sense.'

Declan knew who he wanted to tell.

'Can I say one more thing, Declan?'

'Yeah?'

'You want to teach that kid, so teach him. Don't let those bastards stop you.'

'But what about Tommy? They could hurt him.'

'Then that'd be them and you, wouldn't it?'

'I haven't hurt him.'

'You're his hero, and you push him away. Course it hurts him.'

16

Declan stood at the school gates, looking up and down the road.

'Hi,' said Laura, coming up to him, smiling. 'Waiting for me?'

'But of course. Who else?'

'No, seriously, who are you looking for?'

'Tommy.'

'That makes a change. You spend most of your time trying to avoid him,' she laughed, tossing her hair back with her hand.

'That's the trouble with little red-haired nuisances, isn't it?' said Declan. 'There's never one around when you need one.'

'I'll head in,' Laura said, nodding towards the school.

'I'll hang on until the bell.' Declan watched as she started to walk off. 'You haven't seen Gnasher and Kelz, have you?' he called after her.

'Kelz won't be in till later; she's going up town, shopping for tomorrow night. David should be along in a few minutes; I saw him at the shops.'

Declan turned back. Gnasher was sauntering up the road with a few of his friends. He nodded to Declan as he passed.

'Seen Tommy?'

'Isn't he here?' asked Gnasher. 'He left about fifteen minutes ago.'

'I haven't seen him,' replied Declan.

'He should have been here by now. If I see him, I'll tell him you're looking for him.'

'I doubt he wants to see me, after last night.'

'If you're talking about him saying he wished you'd died, he was really sorry about that when he got home,' said Gnasher. 'He'll be spending all night trying to figure out how to apologise.'

'Tell him he doesn't have to.'

'I'll tell him,' said Gnasher. 'Better still, tell him yourself. Here he is now.'

Declan looked up the road. Tommy was walking along eating a chocolate bar. His school-bag was stuck under one arm, and his shirt was poking out under his jumper.

'You know, I'm sure last time I saw him he was wearing a parka and carrying his dad's sports bag,' said Gnasher. 'Maybe he's flogged them or something. I wouldn't put it past him. He's been acting weird the last couple of days.'

Tommy hurried through the gates, trying not to look at Declan.

'Hi, Tommy.'

'Hi,' mumbled Tommy, without turning around.

'Tommy, can I talk to you for a minute?'

Tommy stopped and turned around.

'I want to say sorry about last night.'

'You don't have to,' said Tommy, looking surprised.

'Yes I do. I was pig ignorant. Doc would never have done that.'

'You're not Doc.'

'No, I know,' said Declan. 'Anyway, if you still want me to coach you I will.'

'That's OK,' said Tommy. 'You don't have to.'

'I know I was bad last night, but I had other stuff on my mind.'

'It's all right, honest. I don't want to put you out.'

'The thing is,' said Declan, 'even if I'm not playing well, I still know how to coach.'

Tommy went quiet.

'Please, Tommy,' said Declan, pretending to beg. 'Just give me a chance; just one time. Just you and me, and if I'm rubbish we'll never have to do it again.'

'When?'

'Well, I'm meeting Laura here tomorrow night at eight. How about before that? Half-seven? Here in the playground, or maybe we can grab a few minutes in the gym before badminton starts.'

'Yeah, OK,' said Tommy, grinning at last. 'It's a deal.'

'Right,' smiled Declan. 'Shake.'

He put out his hand and Tommy shook it.

'I said I'd get you,' he grinned.

'And you did, Mountie.'

'What?'

'It's something my dad says,' Declan explained. 'The Mounties always get their man.'

'Sure,' said Tommy.

Declan walked into class smiling. He sat down by Laura.

'You look like the cat that got the cream,' she whispered. 'Let me guess. You're going to teach Tommy.'

'Yes.'

She squeezed his hand.

'Yuck,' whispered Gnasher from behind them. 'Cut it out, that'll put me off my lunch.'

❑

Tommy checked his watch. Six forty-five; he was meeting Declan in forty-five minutes. He zipped his bag. His basketball gear was in the bottom; on top of it were two old sweaters, a flask of hot water, a small bottle of fresh lemon juice, a tiny jar of honey, a packet of Disprin, a miniature bottle of whiskey, and two cheese sandwiches.

'Right, Mam, I'm off,' he called into the front room.

'Don't be too late back, will you?' his mother called out to him.

'I won't.'

He went out the side door. He was quite looking forward to his practice with Declan, but that was overshadowed by his concern for Billy. Bill hadn't looked well all week. Tommy had taken a couple of days off school — no one had noticed him sneaking out after registration — just to stay with him in his hiding-place on the building site. Billy was running a temperature and sweating. That morning he'd just lain in his sleeping-bag, mumbling. Tommy wondered if he was delirious. He wanted to call an ambulance or a doctor, but Billy had made him promise he wouldn't do either. He didn't want to be found and returned to his father. So Tommy had decided to try and nurse him himself.

He went up the road and stopped at the wild hedge that hid the hole in the fence. There didn't seem to be anybody around. He slipped through the hole in the fence and went towards the small fenced area inside, where Billy was hiding.

'Billy?' he called, starting to squeeze into the gap in the fence. 'Bill —'

A hand grabbed him around the neck and jerked him back out.

Oh, shit! Security!

He was thrown up against the fence, hard.

'We saw you sneaking in here,' sneered Jason Meade, 'and wondered what you were up to.'

'Maybe he's got a little boyfriend in there,' grinned O'Connor.

'Or maybe Billy's a girl, like that singer,' sniggered Cahill.

'I hope so. I haven't had a girl for a couple of hours.' He moved his hips suggestively, and the others laughed.

'Billy's my cat,' Tommy lied. 'He's gone missing, and —'

'Who told you to talk?' said Jason Meade. He put his hand across Tommy's mouth.

'No. It wouldn't be a girl,' he said. ''Cause Tommy's a little fag. He's Donnelly's new boyfriend. Isn't that right, Tommy?'

'Then let's see what you've got, Tom,' laughed Cahill. He grabbed Tommy's testicles and squeezed hard. Tommy felt as if he was going to be sick. Tears jumped out of his eyes.

'If he's hanging around with Donnelly, he's got no idea what a real man's like,' said Meade, grinning at him. 'Maybe I should show him.'

Tommy eyes opened wide. He was shaking. He heard Meade opening the zip on his jeans.

Then something moved behind him, and some sort of liquid whizzed past his ear. Meade yelled, put up his hands and clutched his eyes.

'Run, Tommy,' a voice behind him rasped weakly.

Tommy reacted instinctively. He lashed out with his boot, catching Meade hard between the legs. As he staggered back, Tommy made a run for it.

'Where do you think you're going?' shouted O'Connor, racing after him.

'Even if you get away now, we'll get you later,' Cahill laughed.

They might well have been right, but Tommy wasn't waiting to discuss it with them. He raced across the site, with O'Connor and Cahill close behind him.

He headed for the shell of the building. There was a ladder standing against one of the upright girders, stretching up to what would someday be the third floor. Without thinking, he raced to the ladder and started to climb.

Cahill started to climb after him. 'You're dead,' he called. 'Dead!'

Tommy scrambled on as fast as he could.

'Phil!' he heard Meade call to Cahill. 'Leave that little fucker. We'll get him later.'

'Fair enough.'

Tommy stopped. He looked down.

Oh, God!

The ground was miles away. He quickly looked up again, clinging to the ladder. The ladder began to rock furiously; Cahill was shaking it and laughing.

Tommy stepped onto one of the crossing girders, holding on to an upright for all he was worth. He'd just stepped off the ladder when it went thundering down. It crashed onto the concrete and shattered.

He had no way down.

He slipped slowly into a sitting position on the horizontal girder, clinging to the upright with his arms and legs. His head was spinning. His heart was racing. He couldn't get the thought out of his mind: he could fall at any minute, literally any minute. He was frozen with fear.

He could hear Meade and the others shouting. He forced himself to look across at them. Jason Meade was holding something that looked like a rag doll in his hands, pulling it up off the ground. Tommy heard him yell, 'This little scumbag just threw cold piss in my eyes.'

Billy!

Meade threw Billy against the fence and began pounding him with his fists.

'See what you've got coming, Tommy?' he shouted. The others joined him, kicking Billy to the ground.

Tommy heard Billy moan.

'Bastards!' he screamed, sobbing. 'I'll kill the lot of you.'

17

Declan checked the clock in the car. Twenty-five past seven. He'd waited nearly half an hour. Tommy had obviously decided he wasn't coming. That was fair enough; if their positions were reversed, Declan thought, he'd probably feel the same way. Who wants to be coached by an over-the-hill seventeen-year-old?

He looked in the rear-view mirror. Laura was walking towards the car. They'd decided to meet outside the school after the coaching session. He turned the key in the ignition. Laura opened the door and jumped in.

'Well, how was Tommy?'

'He didn't turn up.'

'Ah, well,' she smiled. 'At least I did.'

'And that's the main thing,' Declan said, returning her smile, as he guided the car out into the traffic. 'Definitely.'

When they reached the Sound Box, Declan parked in a side-street.

'What do you reckon?' he asked. 'Do we have time for a coffee, or should we go in straight away?'

Laura looked at her watch; it was five to eight.

'We don't actually know what time they're on, do we?'

Declan shook his head.

'If we stop off for a coffee we might miss them. So I suppose we should go.'

'Very logical, Miss Byrne.'

'Elementary, my dear Donnelly.'

As they crossed the road to the Sound Box, Laura reached out and took Declan's hand. He liked that. He gave her hand a playful squeeze and she squeezed back.

Laura insisted on paying for herself. Declan accepted that; he didn't have any choice. 'But I'm buying the drinks,' he insisted.

Inside, they saw a few of Gnasher's crowd sitting at a long table. A couple of them looked surprised to see Laura standing by the bar; they were even more surprised when Declan handed her a glass of 7-Up. She saw their surprise and grinned at Declan. 'We seem to have that effect on people, don't we?'

They sat down beside the others. They only had time to exchange a few words before the first band, a bunch of young Iron Maiden wannabes, took to the stage and proceeded to nearly deafen everyone. Next came a synthesiser group, then a rap group. Each band got two numbers.

'The music's certainly got variety,' Declan shouted to Laura, over the sound of some neo-punk band. She nodded back.

Gnasher and Kelz were next. They entered from a side door that led from the dressing-room to the stage. Kelz spotted her friends at the table and smiled. She looked incredibly composed. Declan thought Gnasher looked nervous. His synthesiser was already onstage, and he had a twelve-string guitar slung over his back.

Without any introduction, he pressed a button on the synthesiser. The sound of a snare drum came through the speakers. Gnasher sat down on a stool and began strumming his guitar. Kelz walked up to the mike.

'Boy soldier ...'

Before she'd opened her mouth there'd been some people, particularly at the bar, talking noisily. Within seconds the room was hushed.

When she'd finished, the entire audience applauded hard. Gnasher visibly relaxed.

'Hi,' said Kelz, looking at a spot somewhere at the back of the hall. 'We're called Don't Eat The Donkey Mon.'

A couple of people laughed.

'Hey, don't blame me,' said Kelz, smiling at Gnasher. 'He came up with that.'

Gnasher looked uncomfortable.

'But he also came up with this. It's called "Time and Tide".'

Gnasher put down his guitar and turned to the keyboard. He moved his fingers along the keys. The sound was slow and mystical, like something from an Enya or Clannad album; but gradually that changed into a haunting Celtic melody, played on simple piano. When Kelz joined in her voice was clear and gentle, combining with the melody and lyric to create an effect that had the audience totally hushed.

'You promised me your time,
And willingly did I
Believe
That the time that you had promised me,
Well,
If not all eternity,
Would last as long as we
Should breathe.

But time and tide,
And tide and time,
Are things that we can't hold
And freeze
No matter how we try.

> *Time and tide*
> *And tide and time*
> *Will just roll on and on*
> *And when you look,*
> *Just like your love, they're gone....'*

Declan felt the hairs standing up on the back of his neck as he listened.

When they'd finished, the audience gave them a full three minutes of applause.

The MC bounced on stage, shaking his head and smiling.

'Wow! What a performance. What a voice. What a song. If they don't make it, I *will* eat my donkey. That was Don't Eat The Donkey Mon.'

Declan looked at Laura. She had tears in her eyes.

'I gather you liked that.'

'Amazing.'

A couple of minutes later, Gnasher appeared at the side door and signalled to his friends by raising his hand, miming a cup of coffee, and indicating the far door.

'Anyone going for a coffee?' Declan asked the crowd at the table.

'You joking?' one of the guys replied. 'After what it cost us to get in here, we're staying to see everything,'

'Yeah. Even the guy who sweeps up after the gigs,' laughed one of the girls.

'What about you?' Declan asked Laura. 'Want to stay?'

'It'd be nice to have a cup of coffee and a chat with them, after that. If that's OK with you,' she replied.

'That's just what I was thinking.'

Gnasher and Kelz were sitting in a coffee bar just across the road. They were drinking cappuccino and Kelz was eating a slice of cheesecake.

'What did you think?' she asked excitedly, as Laura and Declan joined them.

'Brilliant,' answered Laura, 'absolutely brilliant. Did you enjoy it?'

'Wow! It was probably the biggest buzz of my life. I'd love to go and do it all again right now.'

'What about you, Dave?' asked Laura.

'I think I'd rather stick to writing,' admitted Gnasher. 'That was a bit nerve-racking for me.'

'But you'd get used to it,' said Kelz. 'You tell him, Declan, he won't believe me.'

'The songs, the music, Kelz's voice — everything was just perfect,' replied Declan. 'I'm sure the more you did it, the more perfect it would get, and your nerves would soon go.'

'Maybe,' said Gnasher, taking a sip of his cappuccino. 'Maybe.' He sounded unconvinced.

They sat in the café for over an hour, drinking coffee and talking. Sometimes, Declan felt like pinching himself to make sure it was really happening, he felt so relaxed and happy. But a couple of times he found himself wondering if they'd all still be there if they knew about That Night.

They dropped Gnasher and Kelz off at Kelz's house. On the way there, they passed Sarah's home. Sarah and Conor were sitting on the low wall around the house. She had her arms around his neck and her head on his shoulder.

'Ain't love grand,' laughed Gnasher.

'They deserve each other,' said Laura.

18

'Declan? Declan!'

Declan was woken by his mother calling him. 'Laura's on the phone. She asked me to wake you. She said it's urgent — something about someone called Tommy.'

Declan jumped out of bed and raced downstairs, taking them two at a time. He picked up the phone in the hall.

'Laura?'

'You didn't by any chance see Tommy on your way home last night, did you?'

'No. Why?'

'He's missing. His dad went up to call him this morning and he wasn't there, his bed hadn't been slept in, and the last thing anyone knew was he was going to meet you.'

'But he didn't turn up. Did they try his pals?'

'Yes, all of them. No one's seen him.'

Declan looked at his watch. 9.00am. 'Hang on, I'll be right over.'

He raced upstairs, got changed, ran back downstairs and picked up the car keys. He poked his head around the door of the kitchen. His mother was there, chatting to his sister Jenny. He nodded to her.

'Is everything OK?' asked Rose.

'Some kid's gone missing. It's probably nothing, but he's a friend's brother, so I'm just going over to see if there's anything I can do.'

He spotted Jenny's mobile phone on the table.

'Can I borrow this? Just in case?'

'Sure,' she answered. 'But I want to hear all about Laura when you get back.'

'Mam, you're an old rogue,' Declan said. Before his mother could reply, he was in the car and on his way.

Five minutes later, he was driving past the school. He turned down past the building site, heading for Laura's house.

Then he stopped. He'd seen Tommy hanging around there a few times lately. *Maybe....* He reversed the car up the road, but didn't go around the corner to the main entrance. He got out of the car and walked over to the place where he'd seen Tommy.

When he looked closely at the hedge, he saw a hole in the fence behind it, hidden by the branches. He scrambled through.

It was Saturday; the site was deserted, closed for the weekend. Declan wandered around.

At one corner of the site, he could see a small compound with containers and pallets inside. A bundle of old rags was lying in front of it. Declan was already turning away when he noticed the rags moving slightly.

It's a person!

He raced over. For a moment of pure panic he thought it was Tommy, but this boy was older, and his hair was fair, not blazing red. The arm sticking out from the parka was hardly more than skin and bone.

Very gently, Declan placed his hand under the boy's head and turned his face to the side. His eyes were closed and bruised. His nose seemed to be broken and his lips were badly cut. His face was covered in dried blood.

Declan placed his hand on the fragile neck, looking for a

pulse. It was there. At least he was alive. Declan knelt beside him, talking to him.

'It's OK. I'm here now. You're going to be OK.' He looked at the thin, wasted little body, almost lifeless, and didn't know if he believed himself. 'You'll be OK.'

He pulled out the phone and dialled Laura's number.

'Hello?'

'Laura, it's Declan. I'm on the building site by the school. There's someone here. It's not Tommy, but whoever he is, he's badly hurt. Can you get someone to help?'

'Sure. I'll be there in a second.'

Declan ended the call.

'They'll be here soon,' he said reassuringly.

The boy raised an arm and tried to lift it over his head.

'Stay still. Someone will be here soon,' said Declan, trying to sound comforting.

The boy raised his arm again and again, gasping. Declan realised he was trying to point to something. He looked around, but there was nothing there. He stared at the shell of the new building.

Then he saw Tommy. Half-sitting, half-slumped on the girders.

Declan heard a sound behind him and turned. Gnasher and Laura were coming though the fence. He could stay with the boy and let Gnasher go and get Tommy, or wait till someone else could.

'Look after him,' he called. He raced towards the building. Tommy was twenty or thirty feet up.

'There's an ambulance on its way,' Laura called after him.

Declan looked up at Tommy. The boy's face was frozen in terror. He recognised the look; his whole body remembered it from that first night. He couldn't leave it to someone else. Doc hadn't left it to someone else to save him, that first night.

He reached the foot of the frame and looked around for

some way to climb. The only ladder he could see was smashed on the concrete. 'Hang on, Tommy. Hang on,' he called. He picked up the pieces of the ladder. They were all useless.

He looked up. The lowest vertical girder was about eighteen inches above his head. He jumped up, caught it, pulled himself up and stood up on the crossbeam. He was going to have to do it the hard way. He caught hold of the upright at a point about ten inches above his head and clung on. He grabbed the side of the girder tightly with his knees and feet and began to haul himself up, monkey-style.

Just like shimmying up one of the ropes in the gym, he told himself. He knew he was lying.

'Tommy. Tommy,' he called, climbing up towards Tommy's right-hand side. 'It's Declan. Hold on tight. I'll be with you in a minute.'

Tommy opened his eyes. They were red from crying, and heavy from lack of sleep. He'd sat there all night, holding on, too scared to sleep in case he fell off. He knew if he waited long enough someone would come. But he hadn't expected this. Meade was coming for him. He could hear him calling.

'Piss off, Meade! Piss off and leave me alone!' Tommy picked up a rivet from a box nearby and threw it down with all his force, clinging on desperately with his other hand. He hated Meade. He wanted him to fall and die. 'Bastard! Scumbag!' He began to throw the rivets down by handfuls.

The rivets sailed past Declan's shoulder. He could hear Tommy howling with fear.

'Tommy, it's not Meade! It's me, Declan,' he called. 'It's me. Stop.'

Tommy could hear Meade perfectly. *'I'm coming to get you, Tommy. It's your turn now. Your turn.'*

'Get lost, Meade. Get lost,' he screamed, hurling handfuls of rivets at the climbing figure. 'Get lost!'

Declan was just below him, and the missiles were getting too close. If one of them struck home he'd be in serious trouble. He could lose his grip and fall.

Tommy was only a few feet above him.

'Look at me. Look at me!' he called, stepping onto a horizontal girder, away from the upright.

He looked straight into Tommy's face. The kid looked exhausted and terrified. His eyes stared at Declan without the slightest hint of recognition.

'Get lost, Meade! Leave me alone!' screamed Tommy.

He lifted a handful of rivets.

Declan had to get away from his throwing hand. He grabbed onto the upright and swung his body behind it, into space, his foot searching for another horizontal girder. He touched it and stopped. He was now directly below and behind Tommy, out of the way of the missiles.

'Tommy, it's Declan,' he called again.

Tommy couldn't turn around. Meade was behind him now, mocking him. He hung onto the beam with his legs and swung his arms behind him. 'Piss off, Meade! Get lost!' He started to fall back, but at the last minute he managed to cling onto the horizontal girder. Now he was lying with his feet clutching onto the upright and his body lying across the horizontal beam.

'Piss off. Leave me alone. Please leave me alone,' he sobbed.

Declan swung himself up so that Tommy's lower body was jammed between him and the girder. He leaned over, grabbed Tommy's shoulder, pulled him into a sitting position and wrapped his arms around him, clutching the girder.

'Please, Jason, don't, please don't,' Tommy sobbed.

'It's OK, Tommy. OK, I've got you now,' Declan whispered, but he knew Tommy didn't hear him. His mind had taken him into some place where the only other person was Jason Meade.

Declan couldn't do anything but wait for someone to help him. So he looked down, thinking, hating the thoughts that were coming into his mind.

He heard the sound of the ambulance and saw it turn onto the site through the main entrance. Two cars followed it, and a couple of men jumped out. One of the men had red hair — probably Tommy's father. Gnasher pointed to the roof.

The men seemed to know what they were doing. They walked back to the entrance of the site and returned carrying long ladders. After a few more seconds, Declan heard the clatter of the ladders being raised. Then the red-haired man appeared at the edge of the roof.

'If you can pass him to me....'

❑

When Declan finally reached the ground, he wasn't just exhausted, he was angry and frightened. He knew who'd done this and why. They'd done it because they could, because no one had ever bothered to stop them, because neither he nor Doc had told anyone about that first night. They'd kept quiet, stuck to the code. So Meade and the others could go for whoever they liked. They could bully little kids like Tommy — bully him so senseless that he could have been killed — and that other poor sod on the floor. It made Declan furious, but it also scared him.

He knew Meade's thinking, knew how much Meade hated him. *Meades aren't allowed to lose....* That was what this was really about; Tommy had just got caught in the middle. He had been getting too friendly with Declan, and so he had to be taught a lesson. The other kid had probably just happened to be in the wrong place. They didn't care who they hurt.

And who'd be next? Kelz, Gnasher, Laura?

Declan couldn't put them at risk. Not after what had happened to Tommy and the kid.

They'd won.

Meade and friends one — Declan loses big-time.

'You OK?' said Laura, putting her arms around him.

He gently moved her arms away.

'Sorry, Laura.'

He looked at her for a second, then turned and walked away.

Then he started running. He couldn't look back. He could imagine the look of confusion in her eyes, but he didn't want to see it.

He got into the car, gunned the engine and drove off before anyone could stop him.

They'd won again.

The tears were falling so hard he couldn't see the road. He pulled over into a side-street.

❏

'What were you running away from?'

He had been standing on the basketball court. Kumar had been standing opposite him, staring at him.

'When you came here, what were you running away from?' Kumar had repeated.

'I don't know what you mean,' Declan had said. 'Everyone knows why I'm here. It was the kids' book. I found it in a second-hand bookshop in Dublin, and I just knew I had to come.'

Kumar had limped up the court, taken the ball out of Declan's hands and put it on the ground.

'That might be the answer to why you're *here*, in this camp in Nepal, but it doesn't answer the real question: *why* you are here.'

'I thought it did.'

'Of course it didn't. Look.'

Kumar had nodded at a group of men sitting in the narrow pathway that ran between the backs of two rows of huts. They'd been drinking beer, cursing and laughing as they gambled; just the sort of thing you'd see in Dublin most Saturday nights.

'They're drinking themselves into oblivion to run away from the fact that they don't have a home or a country any more; that tomorrow they'll be doing exactly the same thing, sitting here in a refugee camp in Nepal, while back in Bhutan their farms, their businesses and their homes are in the hands of people they used to think of as their countrymen. That's what they're running away from. But what about you? What was so terrible that you came half a world away from your family to avoid it?'

'I don't know what you mean.'

'At first I thought maybe it was one of those Irish terrorist things. But that's not you, is it, Declan? So what's got you running? It won't go away, you know. It'll still be there waiting for you when you go back.'

❑

Declan put his hands on the steering-wheel, rested his head on his hands and cried.

19

Declan stood in the back garden, holding the basketball in his hands. He wasn't moving. He was just standing there.

It was the first time he'd been out of his room for a week. He didn't want to see or talk to anyone. His parents had been away all week, visiting his sister Angela in Birmingham — they'd only got back last night — so he'd had no one to make excuses to. He'd just sat there, in the dark, hardly moving. He hadn't even answered the phone.

He wondered what Laura was doing. He could see her in his mind — not the way she'd been when he'd left her standing on the building site, confused and upset, but as she had been all the other times: in the park, in the Sound Box, in the café. Her smile, her laughter. He missed the way she'd made him feel. He missed her. He tried to convince himself it was better like this.

He hadn't answered her calls, but he'd heard her leaving messages on the answering machine. She sounded bewildered and unhappy, but what could he do? It was safer for her this way. Something bad seemed to happen to everyone he got close to. Doc was dead, Tommy could have been killed, so could the other poor kid, and Declan didn't even know him.

He didn't care what Kumar said; he couldn't risk that for Laura and Gnasher.

He knew from Laura's messages that Tommy was OK. He'd told everyone he'd been climbing up the shell of the building and had got stuck when the ladder slipped. He said he hadn't seen what had happened to the other kid.

The kid himself, Billy, was too badly hurt to remember much. His jaw was wired shut, two of his ribs had been broken, and he had a bad case of bronchitis. He'd been in hospital for five days. While he'd been there, his dad had turned up, drunk, threatening the nurses and doctors, insisting that Billy had to be sent home to him. Joe Byrne, Laura's father, had taken him outside to calm him down. No one knew what had been said, but when he was discharged Billy would be going home to the Carolans'. He'd be sharing Tommy's room, and when he was well, he'd be going to school with the rest of them.

Meade hadn't been mentioned.

It made Declan sick to think he was getting away with it again. But there was nothing he could do about it. Nothing. It was better for everyone if he just stayed out of the way.

They'd won again, big-time. No Laura, no Gnasher. He couldn't have anyone. They'd seen to that.

'Declan? You OK, son?'

He felt the hand on his shoulder and jumped in surprise. His father was standing beside him.

'Sorry, Dad. I was miles away.'

'I'd never have guessed.'

Sean sat down on the garden bench, pulled a half-smoked cigarette and a lighter from his shirt pocket and lit up.

'Dad! You know you're —'

'Shh,' his father cautioned, nodding at the window. 'If the Domestic Authority finds out, there'll be hell to pay.'

Declan looked into the kitchen. It was nearly three o'clock. His mother was doing the crossword, while at the same time keeping one eye on the portable television on the breakfast bar.

'You know after your bypass you were told not to do that again.'

'Yeah, I know, but I'm sixty-seven, Dec. I'm hardly going to change now, am I? And anyway,' said Sean with a sly grin, 'the odd cigarette never really hurt anyone.'

'Apart from the people who died of cancer or had their circulation pack up or got heart disease or respiratory disease, you mean?'

'Yeah, apart from those few million it never hurt anybody, did it?'

'When you put it like that, I suppose not, but ...' Declan let the sentence trail off.

'So you were off in Nepal again?'

Declan nodded. It wasn't the truth, but it was easier to explain.

'It's natural,' said his father. 'You haven't been home long. Of course you're going to remember it, and sometimes you'll even see it. It happens to us all. Anything can set it off — a smell, a sound, a thought.'

He took another puff on his cigarette.

'You didn't get out much this week?'

'No, too much homework,' Declan lied.

His father just nodded.

Declan lifted the ball, rested it on the palm of his right hand, and sent it sailing through the hoop screwed onto the back wall of the house, just inches away from the living-room window.

'Darragh says you've given up basketball,' Sean said. 'He says the coach is going mad.'

'Well, he doesn't exactly like the idea.'

'Why'd you give it up, Dec?' asked his father. 'I'm not prying. It's your decision. But you're so bloody good, it seems such a shame not to use that talent.'

He retrieved the ball and tried to copy Declan's movement, but the ball flew out of his hand and slammed against
the window frame.

'It just seems like a waste of time.'

'Is that what you thought when you were out there in the
camp, getting the little kids to play the game and have fun?'
asked his father, going back to the bench.

'No, but that was different. It had a purpose then, but
now ...' Declan shrugged.

He turned away, watching his mother move around the
kitchen. He wished he could tell them the truth. *Dad, Mam,
there's something I want to tell you....*

But he couldn't say it. *That famous fucking code, huh, Doc?*

'Do you know Tom Hyland?' his father suddenly asked,
for no apparent reason.

'You mean the East Timor Group fella?' asked Declan,
surprised.

'The very man,' replied Sean. 'He was a bus driver, same
as me, but since they started the East Timor campaign he's
given himself to it wholeheartedly. But I'll bet you something, son. I bet he hasn't given up the odd game of darts or
snooker, or game of cards, or whatever he did to relax and
enjoy himself.'

He was building his argument carefully, point by point.
'Don't get so caught up in Bhutan that you lose yourself and
have time for nothing else, Dec. If you do, you'll just wear
yourself out, and you'll be no use to anyone.'

'Don't worry. I'll be OK, honest.'

Declan didn't believe it for one minute. He'd started to,
that Friday in the Sound Box with Laura, Gnasher and
Kelz; it had seemed as if everything really could work out
OK. Then it had all fallen apart again.

His father shot another furtive glance towards the window,
fished out another half-smoked cigarette and lit it quickly,
turning his back to the window.

'How many have you got in there?' asked Declan.

His father smiled and took another drag.

'I'll tell you what,' said Declan. 'I'll go back to basketball if you swear to give those things up.' He felt fairly safe making that offer; his father obviously had no intention of giving up.

'Ah-ah,' cautioned Sean, wagging a finger at him playfully. 'I said it was your decision. I wasn't going to interfere. So that's not fair.'

'I didn't say I was being fair, did I?'

'*Touché.*' His dad smiled.

'You know, if I don't start playing again I'll lose my scholarship to the States.'

'We didn't really want you to go anyway. You're a big enough pain already; what'd you be like with a degree in marketing and finance?'

Declan nudged him in the ribs. 'How would you feel about teaching or development work?'

'I think I'm a bit long in the tooth to start studying.'

'No, seriously. How would you feel if I went into something like that?'

'Dec, all we want is for you to be happy. That's all we want for any of you.'

'I was thinking about switching schools.'

'Janey Mack! Where did that come from?' Sean asked in surprise.

'I've been thinking about it for a while,' Declan lied. 'I don't really want to do another two years. I was thinking about maybe going to one of those private colleges where I could do the course in one year.'

'Well, if you're sure that's what you want. I'm sure I can find the money some —'

'No, I don't want you to pay,' said Declan, cutting him off. 'But if you could help me get a loan from the credit union, I could get a part-time job to pay it off.'

'Do you know how much pressure that would put you under, son?'

'I know it'll be hard work, but I can do it. I really want to give it a try.'

'If that's what you want.'

Sean took another drag of his cigarette. Then he put his hand on Declan's knee.

'What's really wrong, Dec?' he asked softly. 'You haven't been yourself since you came back. For a couple of days there, when you went out with Darragh and then you were friendly with that young one, Laura, we thought you were sorted; but now this.... What's up, son?'

'Nothing, Dad, honest,' Dec said. 'Nothing.'

'I wish I could believe you, Dec, but ...' His father stopped. 'You know, whatever it is, we're here for you, and we're too old for anything to shock us any more.'

'Honest.'

'Declan?'

He looked up. His mother was calling him from the back door.

'Visitor.'

'I'm OK, Dad, I promise.' Declan stood up to go. Then he did something he hadn't done for years. He leaned over and kissed his dad on the cheek.

20

Gnasher was standing in the hallway, his hands in the pockets of his jeans.

'How's it going?' he asked, looking straight at Declan. Neither his face nor his voice showed any emotion.

'I'm OK. You?'

Gnasher stared at him. Declan felt him searching his face with his eyes. 'I just turned around, last week, and you were gone. Laura phoned a couple of times and nobody answered. What's the story?' he asked in the same flat tone.

'Just a touch of flu,' said Declan.

'Bull!' Gnasher spat the word out firmly. 'That's pure bull. You know it and I know it. So come on, what's the story, Declan?' he demanded. 'Whatever about me, Laura's got a right to know. She's really upset. She misses you.'

Declan closed his eyes, bit his lip and took a deep breath.

God, how he missed her. He had never wanted to hurt her. He was trying to protect her and the others in the only way he knew how.

He shook his head and opened his eyes. He could feel the tears coming. He couldn't carry on carrying all this around inside him.

'Not here,' he said quietly. 'I'll buy you a pint and we'll talk.'

They drove down to the pub near the school without saying a word. As they walked in, Declan turned to Gnasher.

'You grab a seat and I'll get the drinks. What do you want?'

'Just a coffee.'

Declan ordered the drinks and brought them to the table.

'So, you want to tell me about it? Why the disappearing act? Why did you drop Laura like a hot brick?'

'I didn't drop her,' Declan defended himself.

'Well, that's how it looked from where I was standing.'

'There —'

What Declan was going to say was drowned out by a shout from the other side of the room.

'Hey, Donnelly. I want a word with you.'

He looked up, Meade was walking towards him. Cahill and O'Connor were sitting at a table, watching him.

Declan felt his stomach begin to cramp. He looked at Gnasher. Would he be next?

He had to bluff it out. Either that or fold and run.

'I said I want a word with you,' Meade repeated.

'Well, I'm here, amn't I?' Declan snapped back.

Meade planted his hands on their table and stared aggressively into Declan's face.

'What you been saying about me, Donnelly?'

'Not half as much as I could, Jason,' Declan snapped back.

'I'd watch that mouth. It may be pretty, but it could get you into a lot of trouble,' Meade sneered.

'If you don't mind, we're talking,' said Gnasher, tapping Meade on the hand.

Meade turned and stared at him. 'You're that Coyle kid, with the Mongol sister.'

'The Mongols were a people who invaded Europe around the fifteenth century. Sharon's Down's Syndrome,' said Gnasher.

'Whatever. Do you know what you're sitting with?'

'No, but I know what I'm listening to — a moron.'

'Another big mouth,' sneered Meade.

'I can see you are,' Gnasher snapped back.

'Well, watch your back with this one. He's fucking queer.'

'At least he's not fucking brain-dead like you.'

Meade stormed off.

'I told you. Being an arsehole runs in his family,' said Gnasher.

Declan was shaking. He couldn't look at Gnasher.

'So is that what's keeping you and Laura apart? This "queer" thing they keep throwing around?' As he said the word 'queer' he made quotation-mark signs with his fingers.

Declan nodded 'I suppose that's part of it.'

'Listen, I didn't think you were going to get married. I just thought you could be friends. That shouldn't change it. Just so I know, Dec, *are* you gay?'

'I don't know.'

'How in God's name can you not know? I would have thought it was fairly clear.'

Declan took a deep breath. Then he told Gnasher all about the night they came for him the first time.

'Those bastards,' said Gnasher in disbelief. 'That's rape.'

Declan nodded. He knew it was. Rape didn't have to involve a penis; any forced entry was rape. He'd read that in *Newsweek*.

'God, Dec, I'm really sorry. But I don't see how it makes you gay.'

'When they did it to me, even though it hurt, something happened — you know, physically ... down there.' He nodded at his lap. 'And when Doc put his arm around me, I kind of reacted ... well, you know, the same way again. I didn't mean to. It just happened.'

'And you think that makes you gay?'

'Well ...'

'It was an involuntary reaction, Dec. It doesn't mean a thing.'

'But if that happens, then surely —'

Gnasher cut him off in mid-sentence. 'I work as a volunteer in Amnesty. I've read a lot about male rape. It's used quite often as a weapon of war — disgusting as that is. It's not a sex thing, it's about power. The reaction you're talking about is quite normal. It's a physical, involuntary thing; it comes from the stimulation of a gland. It doesn't imply *anything*. The defence in a recent prison rape case tried to use the fact that the guy got an erection as some sign of consent. The judge laughed it out of court.'

'It's not just that, though,' Declan admitted. 'I just loved being around Doc. I couldn't wait to be close to him. I idolised him. I had other friends, but I just loved being near Doc. Sometimes I'd deliberately change route so I'd pass his house on the way to school, just on the off-chance I might to get walk up with him. Or in school I'd find reasons to be near him, and he never seemed to mind. And after matches we'd always sit together to talk things over, and in the shower I'd always manage to be near him. Sometimes I'd find myself sneaking looks at his body, and once or twice we accidentally touched shoulders or backs and it gave me this great buzz.'

Gnasher looked at him and shook his head slowly, but didn't respond.

'The thing is, I don't know what I'd have done if he'd — done anything. I'd never felt about anyone the way I felt about Doc. In the camp I was close to a guy called Kumar, but that was definitely more of a big-brother thing; and I like Tommy, but that's a little-brother thing....'

'Don't get me wrong,' said Gnasher slowly. 'I'm not saying you're not gay. But that sort of idolisation you were on about — it's a crush. It's normal. Everyone goes through it. Girls just talk about it a lot more than guys. It's not a sign of anything. Have you ever felt like that about anyone else?'

'Up until I met Laura, no.'

'Newsflash. She's female. Dec, I don't know what you are, gay, straight, whatever, but I think you're an OK guy if that means anything. Anyway, more important than how I feel about it, it doesn't matter a shit to Laura. She's not deaf, and Conor's been bad-mouthing you enough for a whole army. She just wants a pal. So don't let those bastards mess with your head. If you're scared of them, that's one thing; but don't let them decide what you are. I mean, look at them.'

Meade and the others were trying to force their way into the company of two fifth-year girls who had come in for a Coke after badminton practice. They were making suggestive remarks at the tops of their voices. The girls looked uncomfortable, and other people in the bar were clearly getting annoyed.

'They're bleeding pathetic.'

Declan smiled. He felt lighter, relieved of a huge burden.

'Can I tell you about something else?' he asked.

'Sure. Doctor Coyle's counselling service, open for business.'

'It's about the Friday before Doc died.'

❑

There isn't any senior basketball practice that night, but Doc and Declan stay back to coach the juniors. When they've all changed and gone, Doc suggests they try a little one-on-one. Then he tries out some new coaching: blindfolding Declan, getting him to shoot from all over the court. Declan takes off his watch and leaves it on a chair.

Finally they decide it's time to hit the showers. They

head for the changing-room, pull off their kit. That's when Declan remembers his watch.

As he opens the door to the gym, he hears a sound out in the changing-room, but it doesn't worry him; he hardly notices it. His watch is on the far side of the gym. It takes him seconds — a minute, tops — to retrieve it. But when he gets back to the door, he hears noises in the changing-room....

❏

Gnasher listened, his face twisting with horror.

'Bastards,' he said softly, when Declan had finished. 'They should be shot.'

He glanced at Meade. For a second Declan thought he was going to scream across the bar at him.

'And that's what's coming between you and Laura?' he said angrily. 'You're a prat, Dec. You really are. You haven't done anything to be ashamed of! Those bastards' — he jerked a thumb towards Meade and his friends — 'they're the ones who did something wrong. They're beneath contempt.'

Declan managed a smile.

'You want my advice?' Gnasher continued. 'Talk to Laura. Tell her everything. Then talk to a counsellor. And when you're ready, stand up to those bastards.'

'There's something else,' said Declan. He looked at the floor, then up at Gnasher.

'Everyone I care about gets hurt by them. First Doc, then Tommy and that poor kid.'

'Tommy? But he was —'

Declan grabbed Gnasher's arm. 'It was them,' he said. 'I don't know what they did, but it was them. Tommy told me, sort of. And I'm scared they'll come for you and Kelz and Laura....'

The rest of that sentence was lost. Gnasher slammed his

coffee mug down on the table so hard it almost cracked. His face was bone-white, and his eyes shone furiously.

'Let them try,' he spat. 'Don't worry about us, Dec. You just talk to Laura, see a counsellor and maybe the police. We can look after ourselves. And anyway, when Tommy's old man hears what happened, I can promise you that bunch of wankers will never bother anyone again.'

Gnasher picked up his cup and downed what was left of his coffee in one. Then he stood up.

'Let's go,' he said. Then, staring directly at Meade across the bar, he raised his voice. 'Something in here stinks.'

21

Declan opened the passenger door. Gnasher climbed in and closed the door behind him. For once he was quiet. Declan turned the key in the ignition and the engine came to life. Suddenly, he was distracted by a commotion outside. He looked out of his window. Meade and the others were being shoved out of the pub by one of the bouncers. They were shouting and swearing at him.

'They can't be let away with all that, you know,' said Gnasher, looking out at them across Declan. Then he turned and looked straight ahead. 'Don't let them chase you away from us, Declan. You're a good guy.'

He pulled out a mobile phone and dialled a number. Declan heard someone answer. 'Hang on,' said Gnasher, and passed the phone to Declan.

Declan put it to his ear. 'Hello?'

'Declan, is that you?'

'Laura.' He felt a lump in his throat.

'Are you OK?'

'Yeah,' he said softly.

'Only — the way you took off last week, and then you wouldn't come to the phone....'

'I'm fine.'

'You weren't mad at me for something, were you?'

'Christ, no, Laura! You're the best thing that's happened to me in years.'

'Good. I was worried I'd done something.'

'No. It was ...' Declan stopped and looked at his watch. 'I'm just going to drop Gnasher off. Can I come up?'

'Sure, I'd love to see you.'

'I'll be there in five minutes. Bye.'

He handed the phone back to Gnasher.

'Good lad,' smiled Gnasher. 'Will you drop me at Kelz's on the way? I want to tell her old man what you said about Tommy and Billy.'

'Sure. And ... and thanks, pal.'

As they drove out of the car park, Meade spotted them. He ran over and lunged at the driver's window, but before he could make contact Declan accelerated into the road. Meade went face-first onto the ground.

'I hope he broke his bleeding neck,' said Gnasher.

As they turned into the estate and drove towards Kelz's house, they saw Conor and Sarah, in exactly the same spot where they'd been a week earlier. She had her arms around his neck and her legs were wrapped around his hips.

'Maybe they're superglued,' offered Gnasher.

They stopped at Kelz's house, and Gnasher got out. He leaned on the car door before closing it.

'Tell her everything,' he advised. 'She'll understand. You did nothing wrong. It was those bastards. You're the victim. And don't worry about them getting back at anyone. Just think about yourself.'

He slammed the door, and Declan drove off.

He shifted uneasily in the seat. He was scared — scared, excited and frightened. He didn't know which feeling was the strongest. He was going to be honest, tell Laura everything and see what happened. Maybe she would walk away in disgust, maybe she wouldn't. He didn't think she would, but you can never be sure how you'll react in any situation until it happens. He'd learnt that, That Night. But he still couldn't wait to see her.

She was waiting outside the house when he pulled up. She moved towards the car and opened the door, smiling. Declan felt like crying.

'Hi —'

Before she could say another word, there was a flurry of activity, and a little girl about nine stuck her head in between them. She had a basketball in her hand.

'Hey! I heard you're a great basketball player. Will you give me a game?'

'I just want to talk to Laura,' said Declan, smiling at her.

'Just a quick game, promise. Laura can join us.'

Laura started to shoo her away. 'Not this time, Katie. Maybe next —'

Declan said suddenly, 'No, it's OK. We'll have a quick game.' It gave him the chance to delay it a bit longer.

Laura looked at him in surprise.

'I know we have a lot to talk about, but we'll go for a walk after this, if that's OK.'

'Sure,' she said, unconvincingly.

As they walked up to the green, Declan saw Gnasher and Kelz coming up the avenue. Gnasher nodded to him.

'Kelz's old man wasn't in.... Go for it.'

They didn't do much playing — just some running with the ball — but Declan enjoyed it. Katie was like the kids in the camp: if she couldn't get the ball fairly, she wasn't averse to a bit of tripping. Laura spent most of the time watching.

Then he heard a slow clapping behind him. He turned. Jason Meade was standing at the edge of the green with Cahill, O'Connor and Rafferty.

Not now. Please, not now.

'Hey, Donnelly,' Meade called.

Declan paid no attention.

'Hey, I'm talking to you.'

Declan still ignored him.

'Is this what you dumped my brother for?' asked Meade, turning to Laura.

'I was never going out with Conor.'

'Do you know what this guy is?' Meade asked aggressively.

'I know he's not a dickhead,' Laura said, turning away.

He grabbed her arms tightly. She winced.

Declan froze. He was vaguely aware of Katie grabbing the ball and running off.

'I said, do you know what he is?' Meade demanded, pushing Laura against the bushes. 'He's a fucking queer. Maybe you'd like to try a real man.' He started to push himself against her. Laura struggled.

'Leave her alone,' shouted Declan.

'I don't think so, hero,' sneered Meade. 'She's here. Just like Doc was. You didn't do anything when I put that big faggot in his place, did you? And you won't do anything now, you little poof.'

Declan felt the pain between his legs and in his stomach. His hands were shaking. He stared at Meade.

'Go on, fuck off, just like you did before,' shouted Cahill. He turned and shared a high five with O'Connor.

Declan turned and started to walk to his car. If he left, maybe they'd leave her alone.

'I said, do you want a real man?' repeated Meade, pushing his face so close to Laura's that their noses almost touched.

'If I do I'll ask you, Jason,' said Laura. Declan looked back. She was laughing.

'Now you're talking,' said Meade.

'Yeah,' Laura repeated, still looking at Declan. 'I'll ask you and you can send for Declan.

'Little bitch,' said Meade. 'But I like a woman with fight.'

He pushed his face against Laura's, trying to kiss her. She struggled to pull away, but his grip on her arms was too tight.

Declan felt as if he was watching someone else. It happened so quickly, yet it all seemed to be in slow motion. One minute he was watching Meade pinning Laura against the bushes, pushing his face into hers. The next, he was flinging himself at Meade so hard that he sent him sprawling onto the ground. The others moved in towards him. Declan dived at O'Connor and head-butted him; he went down holding his nose and screaming. Declan turned just in time to see Cahill lunging towards him. He brought up his foot and kicked Cahill between the legs so hard that he almost turned blue. He turned and glared at Don Rafferty, who was standing at the edge of the grass. He motioned for him to come forward but Rafferty backed off, waving his hands. 'No quarrel, Dec, no quarrel.'

Declan wasn't interested in him anyway.

Meade was trying to push himself up. Declan swung at him with both fists closed together. He caught him on the cheek and Meade went sprawling to the ground, landing on his back. Declan knelt over him, pinning Meade's arms to the ground with his knees, and punched away at him in blind fury.

'This is for Doc,' he screamed as he battered him, 'and this is for me. For the thirteen-year-old kid you fucking destroyed, you worthless piece of shit.'

He punched and punched at Meade's face. Meade tried to scream 'I give in,' but Declan wasn't interested. Meade hadn't stopped when that thirteen-year-old kid screamed. He hadn't stopped when Doc cried out. He hadn't stopped when Cahill and O'Connor had been shoving Declan around the changing-room, kicking him in the testicles and banging his head against the wall. He hadn't stopped when Tommy cried out in fear or when that other kid begged them to stop. Declan wasn't going to stop now.

There was blood all over Meade's face. Declan saw it, but he didn't care. He'd gone beyond care. He just wanted to hurt Meade, hurt him as much as he'd hurt the others, as much as he would hurt Laura and Gnasher if he wasn't stopped....

He heard Laura screaming. Hands were dragging him off, but he didn't care. He tried to struggle free. He just wanted to keep hitting, hitting with every ounce of pain and anger and fear and contempt in his body, until he'd punched himself so exhausted that nothing mattered. He was still screaming as they hauled him away.

'I'll kill you, you bastard! I'll kill you!'

Joe Byrne, Laura's father, dragged him into their house and threw him hard into a chair.

'You little psycho!' he yelled, his face red with anger. 'What were you doing? Trying to kill him? Declan, you could have —'

'They raped Doc,' Declan sobbed, breaking down and crying like he'd never cried before. 'Those bastards raped Doc.'

And it just came out, in one long stream of sobs.

'They raped him in front of me, in the changing-room. When I came in, O'Connor and Cahill were holding him bent over the benches. Meade's trousers were down by his knees and he was — he was raping Doc. I was too scared to do anything. All I could was stand there and shake and remember how they'd hurt me. How they shoved that aerosol inside me and squeezed my ... my testicles while they laughed. I was too scared to do anything, and those bastards raped him. And I saw his eyes. He was begging me to help him. And I couldn't move. I could feel the pain of what they'd done to me before, all through my stomach and between ... between my legs — it was like I was on fire.... I wanted to go to him but I couldn't. I couldn't move. And they raped him. And then when I did move, I tried to run away, but they caught me. I fought like mad, but they beat me, they kicked me in between the legs and punched me in the face, and they just kept beating until they heard someone coming....'

Laura's mother wrapped her arms around him and held him as he wept, held him like a baby.

'And I did nothing to help him, and Doc died. He died because of me. And then they beat Billy senseless and went after Tommy....'

He had no idea how long she held him. It could have been minutes or hours. When he looked up, Laura was there beside him.

'That's why I ran, Laura,' he sobbed. 'I was so ashamed. Of what I'd done. Of the way I'd left Doc. Of the way he looked at me afterwards — knowing I'd betrayed him.... Of Billy lying there half-dead, Tommy terrified out of his wits. I was scared they'd come for you and Gnasher next. Don't hate me. Please don't hate me.'

Laura was crying.

'Declan, you're a victim too,' said Chris Byrne softly. 'You didn't do anything wrong. They did.'

'But I betrayed Doc....'

'No,' she said softly. 'Your fear betrayed you both. And they were the cause of that fear — what they'd done to you before. If he'd lived, Doc would have realised that. He was a good boy.'

'But I killed him —'

'No. The Saturday before he died, they were calling him names and threatening him. Sharon Coyle saw them. She told me at the shops that "bad boys" had told Doc "See you next week," and she asked me why it frightened him. I didn't know then. That car crash was an accident, but if something was preying on his mind and distracted him, it was them and not you. You did nothing wrong. You're a victim too.'

Victim. Declan had never liked the sound of the word, but suddenly it was a liberation. He'd done nothing wrong.

'Look, we'd better get you home,' said Chris Byrne. 'I'll just make you a cup of tea to calm you down. Laura will stay with you.'

Laura sat on the floor, holding Declan's hand. They didn't speak. They didn't need to. Their tears said it all.

There was a ring at the door, and Declan heard a man's voice shouting angrily.

'I'll prosecute, I will! For what that little savage did to Jason, I'll see him jailed. The scumbag!'

Then he heard Joe Byrne, speaking firmly but softly. 'I'd think about that. After what we've just heard, I think it would be unwise. Also, I think it's highly probable that your son will soon be prosecuted for some very serious sexual assaults.'

'Don't be preposterous!'

'We'll see how preposterous the guards feel his statement is.'

Then the door slammed shut.

Laura and Declan still didn't talk; being close was all they needed.

When Chris Byrne came back with the tea, Declan took a cup and sipped at it.

'Declan,' she said softly, 'I've worked with women who've been abused. It's not my area of expertise, but I'd like you to call this number sometime. They can help.'

She handed him a slip of paper. Declan slipped it into his pocket.

It took him two days to get up the courage to phone the number. When he did, he heard the words that he hoped might help him to put his life back together.

'Good afternoon. The Rape Crisis Centre.'

Epilogue

Declan slumped back in the chair. He'd felt his shoulders and chest tensing as he told the story, but now it was out he could relax a little.

'And that brings us to where we are now, I suppose.'

'Well, Declan, you've certainly travelled a hard road,' said the counsellor. She smiled reassuringly as she looked across at him. 'Where would you like to go from here?'

'I want to stop being a victim and start being a survivor. To take back control of my life, not give it to them.'

'You've just taken the first step, then, haven't you? I won't promise you an easy journey, but if you want to take it, I'll be here to go along with you.'

'I'd like that. I need it.'

'Well, then let's make another appointment for early next week, OK?'

'OK.'

Declan went back into the reception area of the Rape Crisis Centre. Laura was waiting for him, dressed in jeans and sweatshirt and combat jacket. She smiled and stood up.

'Well?' she asked. 'How'd it go?'

'Better than I'd hoped,' said Declan.

'That's good,' said Laura, as they stepped out into the afternoon rain. 'I won't press it.'

'God, I could do with a coffee.' Declan put his arm around her. 'It was hard, going through all that again, but ...' He took a deep breath and sighed. 'It'll be worth it. To be free.'

They headed down to Stephen's Green, holding hands.

'What are you running away from, Declan?' asked a voice in his memory.

Nothing, Kumar, he thought. *Not any more.*

And for a second he was back in the camp, on his basketball court.

'But when you all started that march to the border, back in 1993, weren't you frightened of what would happen when you reached there? Weren't you afraid that you'd be arrested, beaten, thrown in jail, tortured?'

Kumar had smiled. 'We didn't really think about that. We just started with one step, and then kept going, a step at a time. We couldn't think about the past, because it was over, or about the future, because we didn't know what it would bring. So we just took one step at a time, and waited to see where it would lead us.'

'Fear is a habit. I am not afraid.'

Aung Sun Suu Kyi, Burmese opposition leader,
Nobel Peace Prize winner 1992, Freeperson of Dublin 2000

Author's Note

The title of this book comes from the title of Richie J. McMullen's 1990 book, *Male Rape: Breaking the Silence on the Last Taboo*. My *Breaking the Silence*, however, is a work of fiction. The characters in it are not real — but the situations portrayed are based on fact. Male-on-male rapes and sexual assaults, such as those perpetrated on my characters Declan and Doc, do occur, and with greater frequency than most of us realise. And a hundred thousand southern Bhutanese have lost their lands, livelihood and nationality since 1990. Yet most of us know little about either subject.

It was not until I met Mary Coughlan in the course of my research for *Is Anybody Listening?* that I became aware of the plight of the southern Bhutanese refugees. Similarly, while I was aware of the crime of male rape, it was not until I saw the excellent documentary *Male Rape*, produced by Scratch Films and shown on RTÉ in January 1996, that I became aware of the extent and the devastating effects of this crime.

Male Rape — What to Do

If you are sexually assaulted or raped, remember: it is *never* your fault. You are not responsible for someone else's actions. Young or old, male or female, gay or straight, conservatively or outrageously dressed, *you did not invite the rape*. You are not to blame.

Do seek help for the physical and emotional aftermath of the attack. As well as close contacts such as parents, friends and doctors, there are bodies specifically geared to deal with the problem. This list of useful contact numbers does not claim to be comprehensive:

Samaritans: (1850) 60 90 90
Victim Support: (1800) 66 17 71
CARI: (01) 830 8529
Childline: (1800) 66 66 66
Rape Crisis Centre: (1800) 77 88 88
Your local Garda station

With the exception of www.drcc.ie, which is the site of the Dublin Rape Crisis Centre, all sites listed below are based outside Ireland.

www.drcc.ie
www.igc.apc.org
www.callrape.com
www.rapescrisiscentre.com
www.abuse.recovery.uk
www.rapenetwork.com

Bhutanese Refugees

In 1990, the Bhutanese government began a campaign of intimidation against southern Bhutanese of Nepali origin — revoking their citizenship, confiscating property, imposing the northern Bhutanese culture throughout the country. This set in motion an exodus: an estimated 100,000 southern Bhutanese lost their homes, lands, livelihoods and country between 1990 and 2001, fleeing to refugee camps in Nepal. Of these, not a single person has yet been allowed home. The governments of Bhutan and Nepal have met ten times at a ministerial level to try to resolve the problem; during the tenth round of talks, they agreed to begin a process of verification of the camp population. This development has given the refugees some hope that their aspiration to return to their homes in Bhutan may become a reality.

At the time of writing, the Joint Verification Team of Nepalese and Bhutanese officials has visited the camps in south-eastern Nepal. The actual verification will begin soon.

While the verification process is welcome, many are concerned that so far there is no neutral third party involved. This calls into question the impartiality of the whole process, and raises fears that refugees may be deprived of their rights.

Those wishing to find out more about this situation can consult the following websites:

www.bhootan.org

www.kuensel.com.bt (the site of Bhutan's official newspaper)

The Ireland-Southern Bhutanese Refugee Support Group can be contacted at: mclan@gofree.indigo.ie

Amnesty International is an invaluable source of information for anyone interested in reading more about the abuse of human rights worldwide. The web address for Amnesty International (Ireland) is:

www.amnesty.ie

The book *I See Bhutan In My Dreams* was produced in a limited print run of five hundred, which is now completely sold out. It is, unfortunately, no longer available. However, the Ireland-Southern Bhutanese Refugee Support Group may know of individuals willing to loan their copies to educational institutions on a short-term basis. I have one copy, which I am prepared to make available on such a basis.

Acknowledgements

I would like to acknowledge the help and support of a number of people in making this book possible: Mary Coughlan of the Irish-Southern Bhutanese Refugee Support Group, for introducing me to *I See Bhutan In My Dreams*, the book that proved the starting point for this novel; Angela McCarthy, Head of Training at the Dublin Rape Crisis Centre, for her time and knowledge; Pierce Feirteir, Liz Morris, Aislinn O'Loughlin and Nuala Lyons, for their comments; Monica, for her unconditional but not uncritical support; Eilís French, editor and honorary fifth daughter, for effort above and beyond the call of etc.; and Seamus Cashman, for taking the risk.

Any shortcomings in this book are mine.

Larry O'Loughlin

Also from Wolfhound Press

Is Anybody Listening?

by Larry O'Loughlin

'Sanjid — my name is Sanjid. Is anybody listening?'

When Laura first hears the voices, she thinks she's going mad.
The truth is almost as frightening.

Two children half a world away — Sanjid, an Indian carpet slave,
and Rosa, a Brazilian slum teenager — are calling to her.
Both are helpless. Both are in danger.
Both desperately need Laura's help.

They're ruining her life. Her so-called best friends think she's
weird; her teacher thinks she's on drugs.
Listening to the voices means putting her life in danger.
Refusing to listen means leaving Sanjid and Rosa to die.

The powerful, disturbing story of one girl who hears a cry for
help — and refuses to turn away.

'A heartfelt plea for global justice, underpinned by a compelling
narrative.'
Brian O'Mahony, *The Examiner*

'A powerful, emotional story, told with a sense of urgency
and mounting excitement.'
Robert Dunbar, reviewer

ISBN 0-86327-721-7

Also from Wolfhound Press

Silent Stones

by Mark O'Sullivan

On the farm of Cloghercree stands an ancient circle of stones....

Mayfly is there because her New-Age-traveller parents believe
the standing stones will miraculously cure her dying mother.
Robby is there because, trapped between his embittered great-
uncle and the shadow of his dead IRA father, he can't escape.

But then Cloghercree is invaded by the ruthless terrorist Razor
McCabe, on the run from the police.
And as the shadows of the past begin to close in on them,
Robby and Mayfly know their time together is running out....

By turns gripping, thought-provoking and deeply moving,
Silent Stones is the story of two teenagers forced to come to
terms with their own and their families' pasts.

ISBN 0-86327-722-5